Snowbird Season

Also by BJ Phillips

Seasons
Hurricane Season

Snowbird Season

By

BJ Phillips

Desert Palm Press

Snowbird Season

(Seasons – Book 2)

by BJ Phillips

© 2017 by BJ Phillips

ISBN (trade): 9781942976431
ISBN (epub): 9781942976448
ISBN (pdf): 9781942976455

Desert Palm Press
1961 Main Street, Suite 220
Watsonville, California 95076
www.desertpalmpress.com

Editor: Mary Hettel
Cover Design: eeboxWORX (https://mich-bro.myportfolio.com/projects)

Printed in the United States of America
First Edition June 2017

Acknowledgements

Once again, I must thank my publisher, Lee Fitzsimmons at Desert Palm Press, for still believing the stories I write are publishable. Mary Hettel, this book would not be quite what it is without your great editing skills (and those wonderful cookies you send me). And Mich Brodeur, thank you for another lovely cover. It's a blessing to work with each of you again. We make a great team!

Dedication

This book, as the last one, is dedicated to my wonderful partner, Debbie Hilliard. Your encouragement makes it possible for me to continue to do what I love doing. Thank you so much for continuing to believe in me.

PROLOGUE

KELLY BRADLEY STOOD ON a secluded beach on Sanibel Island watching her friends, Shawn and Carrie, as they exchanged their wedding vows—promising to love each other forever. A bit of her heart was jealous. Yes, she still had a crush on Carrie. She knew from the start that it was pointless to hope for anything more than friendship. Carrie's heart belonged to Shawn from the day they met. Kelly knew they belonged together and was very happy for them.

Still, the romantic in Kelly hoped to find a wonderful, unconditional love of her own. Carrie had called her a knight in shining armor, coming to her rescue. Someday Kelly knew she'd find her own damsel—in distress or not.

CHAPTER ONE

KELLY BRADLEY'S PHONE BUZZED just as she finally sat down for a breather. It was Friday morning and she'd been working out in the carport on the front hall stair bannister. The lack of air conditioning didn't bother her much—she was used to being hot and sticky while working. Florida could be like that, sometimes even this far into autumn.

She took a sip of ice water from her insulated jug, answering the call without looking to see who it was. "Hi, this is Kelly."

"Hey, Kelly. It's Carrie. How busy are you?"

Good thing she'd already swallowed. The sound of that voice always sent her into a little tizzy before she reminded herself that Carrie was her best friend's wife. She took a deep breath and ignored it. "A bit busy, but for you, anything. What's up?"

"It's not for me, personally. It's for Gladstone Construction this time. We have a customer who needs some custom woodworking done. We're up to our eyeballs here and I thought of you. I know you're very picky about the jobs you take, but could you look at this one for me? She needs some custom bookcases built and installed."

"I don't know..." Kelly began running her fingers through her short, sun streaked dark blonde hair.

"I don't think this would take you a long time to do, but it'd be months before we could even think of getting anyone out there to do it. She's one of our favorite customers and we usually handle everything for her as a courtesy. This time, though, she needs them done sooner than we could get to them."

"Let me guess, a snowbird job." The snowbirds she referred to were the people from 'Up North' who came to Florida in fall to escape the winter weather, and returned to their northern homes in the spring. Kelly laughed, wiping her forehead with the back of her hand. "Snowbirds always seem to need things done in a hurry."

"How did you guess? Yes, it is." Carrie laughed. "Listen, she's a nice woman and she's always willing to pay well for top quality work. I am hoping you'll look at it and at least see if it's something you'd like to do. She'd be very grateful if you took it on."

"Right. Well, okay, I'll run out and look at it. I'm kind of burned out on this staircase right now anyway, and could use a break." She stood up, stretching her back.

"I do appreciate this. Thank you so much in advance, even if you don't take the job. I'll text you her contact information and you can call her yourself and set it up. How's that?"

"You know I can't say no to you." Kelly reached for her water jug again. "Send it on over and I promise I'll go take a look. I'm warning you ahead of time, if it's someone wanting a bunch of boards put up on a wall, you know that's not my thing." She took another cooling swig of ice water.

"And you know I wouldn't send you a job like that, right? Besides, she wants some built-in bookcases that look like they've always been there. More like furniture. That sounds more like something you'd do, doesn't it?"

"True, it does," Kelly said. "All right. I'll call her. What's her name, by the way?"

"Elise. Her name is Elise Wainwright. I'll let her know to expect a call from you." Relief was evident in her voice. "Thanks again. You're awesome."

Kelly laughed. "You've said thank you several times now, so you can stop. And you're welcome, already. I'll go out there and talk to Ms. Wainwright, I promise. I'll call her this afternoon."

"Great. I'll let her know. Catch you later? And by later, let's see you sooner rather than later. We haven't seen your face in a bit and we miss it. And bring Piper with you. She's my girl, too."

"Sometimes I believe you like that little mutt better than me, but that's okay. You can always lure me in with one of those famous pies of yours. Just let me know when you bake the next one and I'll be there for sure. My mouth waters even thinking of it. I'm sure Piper misses you, too, as well as all those treats you always have for her. Say hi to Shawn. See you guys soon."

Kelly hit end on her phone and stuffed it into her cargo shorts pocket. She whistled to the small white and brown dog of indeterminate breed playing with a gecko in the breezeway. Piper came running with her tail wagging and Kelly leaned down as Piper jumped into her outstretched arms. Piper began licking her face all over as Kelly carried her into the house.

"You're my girl. Yes, you are." She laughed. "Looks like we're going to visit Aunt Shawn and Aunt Carrie again soon and Aunt Carrie will take you off and spoil you with roast beef for dinner. But don't you forget now, who your mom is. Who lets you sleep on her bed and sit in her chair with her? Me." Kelly laughed again as Piper decided to give her more kisses while she scratched her ears.

She didn't need to check her T-shirt to know she'd better get cleaned up before she called on someone named Elise. Her house was probably spotless, more than likely due to a housekeeper. She sighed. Another rich lady wanting some work done. Well, she could do bookcases if she needed to, since it was for Carrie. How bad could that be? Besides, she could always say no...sure she could.

CHAPTER TWO

KELLY DROVE UP TO the security gate at Palm Harbour Isles, and was glad she'd gotten cleaned up and put on a pair of her better shorts and a polo shirt. She gave her name to the security guard, who found her on the admit list. At least the prospective customer remembered to do that.

The guard asked to see her identification, then wrote her information on a clipboard and handed her a cardboard contractor placard with the date on it for her to put on her dashboard. It was obvious the security officer was used to contractors coming and going all the time for something—lawn service if nothing else. She doubted any of the residents in this upscale neighborhood would dirty their hands to even mow their own lawn. That worked out nicely, since it meant lots of people had jobs.

Once inside the security gate, she drove past sprawling, pastel colored homes with circular driveways. Perfectly manicured lawns displayed magnolias and palm trees sparkling from a light rain half an hour earlier. She took deep breaths to enjoy the fresh aroma of wet grass and leaves as she scanned the numbers on each unique mailbox for her destination address on Gulf Breeze Way. Turning into her potential customer's long, U-shaped driveway, she noticed someone dressed in coveralls out on the front lawn removing some of the lower fronds of a palm tree with a pole saw. Assuming it was the gardener, Kelly stepped up to the front door and rang the doorbell.

She waited for a minute or so, but no one answered. She knew Ms. Wainwright was expecting her, so she rang the bell again. While she waited the second time, she turned around to see the gardener walking toward her, waving.

"Hello there!" The gardener was a woman, coveralls covering most of her. With short greying hair and sparkling blue eyes, she appeared to be in her sixties. "Are you Kelly?"

"Hi. That would be me. Is Ms. Wainwright not at home?"

"Hi Kelly, I'm Elise Wainwright." She laughed a little as she put down the pole saw and took off her leather gloves, then reached out to shake hands. "You look a bit shocked. I get that a lot."

"Hi Ms. Wainwright. I'd say I'm surprised, anyway. I didn't expect to find the owner out in the yard cutting palm fronds. You look like you know your way around yard equipment."

"That I do and please call me Elise. I like working in my own yard whenever I can. I do apologize for not meeting you at the door. Time got away from me." She stomped some of the wet sand off her brown work boots, opened the door, and motioned for Kelly to follow her in. She bent down to loosen her laces enough to step out of the still sandy boots, leaving them and her socks inside on the tile floor by the door. She unzipped the coveralls, stepping out of them and dropping them on the floor next to the boots, revealing a pair of Bermuda shorts and a T-shirt that said *I heart NY*. "Can I get you something? Personally, I could use a big glass of ice water right now. Will you join me?"

"I'd be pleased to, thanks."

Kelly followed Elise through the entry way and the living room to the lanai. Elise opened the sliding glass doors etched with a single palm tree apiece and motioned for Kelly to go through. "If you wouldn't mind, please make yourself comfortable out here and I'll be right back."

Once alone, Kelly took in the large screened and glassed-in lanai, with its big potted birds of paradise, palms, and bromeliads. The natural bamboo furniture with tropical printed cushions completed the look. She walked over to the windows to take in the view of a large yard with the ubiquitous caged pool. Everything was spotless and each item was where it was meant to be, like it dropped down right out of *Southern Living* magazine into the lanai and yard.

"Nice view, isn't it?" Elise's voice startled Kelly out of her contemplation. "I'm sorry. I didn't mean to sneak up on you. I guess I don't make much noise barefooted on these tile floors."

Elise handed Kelly an already sweating iced tea glass full of water and ice cubes.

"Thanks. I was admiring your yard, as you guessed. You must have great staff to keep your place this nice."

"Actually, my 'staff' as you put it, is me. I do have some help come in a couple of times each month to do things I don't have time for, but it's mostly me. I like my privacy, but more than that, I love working in the yard."

"Don't blame you for that. So, Carrie at Gladstone Construction says you need some bookcases. What are you looking for? I mean, open shelves, cabinets in part of them, or what?"

"Tell you what, let's go to the office and I'll show you where I want them. I'm sure you'll have some ideas for designing them. Carrie told me you do a lot of woodworking and that you're meticulous with the pieces you take on." She sipped from her water as she led the way down the hall.

Kelly grinned. "Yes, I am particular when it comes to my work. I don't do a lot of contract jobs because I remodel houses for a living. The typical job I agree to is something that's a bit different. I don't stick up some shelves on L-brackets on the wall. I can see you're not the 'stick up some shelves' kind of woman, though."

Elise grinned back. "No, I'm not. I'd like these bookcases to be built-in furniture. They don't have to be done overnight, obviously, but I'd like them installed before I need to go back to New York in November." She stopped in front of a set of double doors. "Here we are." She pushed both doors open at once, one with her free hand and the other with one of her bare feet.

The doors opened into a substantial room with a wall of windows and French doors opening into a side garden. A large white painted desk took up the center of the room, with a matching credenza behind it. That this was a working office was obvious from the all-in-one printer/fax on the credenza and the paperwork neatly spread on the desk next to the laptop.

"What an attractive office. Yours, I assume."

"Yes, it is. I work here whenever I'm not in New York. I can justify spending more time here if I can get some work done. Besides, it's much nicer to be here than in New York in winter, at least part of it. I'd miss Christmas without snow, so I always go back for the holiday."

"If you don't mind my asking, what do you do?"

"I'm an editor, but I write as well. I'm with a publishing house in New York, so it's easy to bring my work with me."

"I have a good friend who's an author. She says writers can write almost anywhere. This place looks like a perfect place to work as it is. Are you sure you want bookcases in here?"

"I'm sure. I'd love to spend more time here and sometime soon make this my permanent home. I'll keep a small place in New York to stay in when I need or want to go back. I own a rather extensive book collection and I'd like to move most of it here. What about over there? I'm thinking that would make a great library wall." She indicated the wall opposite her desk. It currently sported two comfortable-looking chairs with a lamp table between them and a painting hanging behind the lamp.

Kelly contemplated the scene before her for a minute. "You do want to keep those chairs and the table in here, right?"

"I'd like to. What do you think?"

"Well, you have plenty of floor space in here to move the chairs farther into the room. You could put in the bookcases, with doors on the bottom sections. That would make it work better. I'm assuming you want to keep the colors light in here, like your desk and everything else...not cherry or walnut or the like."

"Exactly. I was thinking that I'd like them painted or stained white, if we can do that. I still want to use furniture-grade wood, not some cheap stuff, even though the wood itself wouldn't be the highlight of the pieces."

"Hmm...I'm getting a couple of ideas. Tell you what, how about if I..."

Kelly was interrupted by the appearance of another barefooted woman in the doorway. She seemed to appear out of thin air and just stood there. She looked to be in her late thirties—about the same age as Kelly, but roughly half a head shorter than Kelly's five foot nine.

Wow, Kelly thought. *That woman is stunning.*

She locked eyes with Kelly for a moment. Without speaking to Kelly, she turned to look at Elise. "Aunt Elise, where would you like me to put the wine for tonight's dinner? I left it on the counter in the kitchen, but if it's supposed to be in the wine cooler or the pantry, I can put it away."

"You can leave it and I'll put it away after we're finished here. Andrea, meet Kelly. Kelly, this is my niece, Andrea. She's spending a few weeks with me."

Kelly smiled and said hi as Andrea looked back at her. There was no response from Andrea, except that she kept looking at her like she was mesmerized. Kelly wanted to look away, but she couldn't stop looking into those eyes.

If Elise noticed Andrea and Kelly still staring at each other, she didn't acknowledge it. She kept talking, apparently oblivious to the looks they exchanged.

"Andrea, I'm trying to talk Kelly into designing and building my new bookcases." Elise turned to Kelly, "What do you think? Is this a job you have time for or want to take on?"

"Nice to meet you, Andrea." Kelly forced herself to look back at

Elise. "Sure, I can do this. I'll need to take some pictures and measurements and I can get back to you in a few days with a preliminary design. After we agree on a design, I can give you a price and I'll make the working drawings. I assume you'll want it to be the same general style as your desk so it looks like it all came together at the same time, right?"

"That's exactly what I want. Okay, I'll leave you to it. I'll be in the kitchen. Back in the same direction as the lanai. Come on in there once you're finished."

"I can do that. I need to run out to my truck and get a few things. Is it all right to let myself back in?"

"Of course, help yourself. See you in a bit, then."

Elise left the room with her arm around Andrea, but Kelly noticed Andrea took one little look back over her shoulder toward her as they left.

What happened there? She didn't offer to shake hands when we met or even say hello but after all, I'm hired help. Maybe she doesn't shake hands with the hired help. Who knows? Anyway, I've got measurements to take.

Half an hour later, photos taken and measurements written into her notebook, Kelly made her way to the kitchen to find Elise and Andrea sitting in a small built-in dinette booth in an alcove. They appeared to be deep in conversation, but both looked up as she intentionally made some noise coming into the room.

"I have a couple more questions for you," Kelly said to Elise. "Do you want to be able to adjust the shelves or do you want them stationary?"

"Hmm...I'd like them to be stationary."

"Okay, do you want them to go to the ceiling or do you want room to put things on top of them?"

"I'd like them all the way to the ceiling. I'll need the entire space for my things. I'll get a library ladder later if it turns out I need one."

"All right, I'll make them far enough apart for you to put some taller books and items in them. I'll start working on a design and give you a call to set up a time to bring you what I come up with in the next few days, if that's agreeable." She tried not to look at Andrea.

"Perfect. Thanks for agreeing to do this. Carrie told me you do amazing things with wood, so I look forward to seeing your design. Can you give me a ballpark figure for this project yet?"

"I'd say it's going to run approximately $4,000, but I can be more precise after we agree on a design. You'll have 19 wall-feet of bookcases, plus they're taller than usual and the bottom couple of shelves are enclosed. Is that in the range you're happy with, price-wise?"

"Since I've looked at some pre-made cabinets I didn't like that cost at least that much, yes, I'm very happy with that price." Elise reached out to shake hands.

"Good. I'll call you soon." She reached to shake Elise's hand and then looked at Andrea. "Nice to meet you, too."

Without waiting for a response, she turned and headed for the door. Once outside, she took a deep breath and shook her head. Andrea seemed to be a total ice queen, but a stunning one. Oh well, she wasn't going to have to be friends with her, just work there. Her aunt made up for it with her warmth.

Once out the front gate and past the security shack at Palm Harbour, she decided to drive over to Carrie's office to tell her she was taking the job. A short while later, Kelly walked through the construction office's front door.

"Kelly!" Carrie jumped up and hurried around her desk to give her a hug. "It seems like ages since I've seen you." Carrie stepped back from Kelly's warm embrace.

"I know. I've been busy with this renovation. I knew taking on a two-story house with bannisters and stairs would mean tons of woodworking. It's taking more time than I first estimated, but I want them to be right. Anyway, I decided to come in person to tell you that I am taking on the Wainwright job."

"Oh, good. Thanks for letting me know. I'm glad you could do it for us and Rich will be glad to know she's in good hands."

"You're welcome. Oh, and you're right, she's a very pleasant woman. From what I've seen, she'll be easy to work with."

"I assumed you'd hit it off. I've always liked her." Carrie looked toward the hall next to her desk. "I was getting ready to take a little break. Come on back to the coffee room and tell me all about your meeting with her. How's our little girl, by the way?"

Kelly followed Carrie around the corner. "Piper's doing fine, as usual. I'm sure she misses you, with all the spoiling you do. It's hard for me to compete when you give her roast beef every time. What do you do, save it for her visits?"

Carrie laughed. "Actually, I do. Whenever I have some left-over roast, I chop it up and put it and a little gravy in a baggie and freeze it for her. It's easy to defrost and makes me very popular. I want to be the favorite aunt, of course."

"I'm pretty sure you already are. All I have to say is 'Aunt Carrie' to her and she starts spinning around like a crazy girl."

"Good. That means it's working." Carrie grinned. "So, give me the lowdown on your meeting with Elise."

"Well, she wants a whole wall of permanently bookcases attached to the wall—built-ins, if you will. She wants them to look like the rest of her office furniture. She's leaving the design up to me, but I'll give her a couple of options and let her decide what she wants. I won't give her anything I don't like, though."

Carrie grinned at her. "No, of course not."

"This should be a much more interesting project than I supposed it would be when I talked to you. By the way, have you met her niece, Andrea?"

"Oh, no, I haven't. I know Elise has a brother and that he and his wife have at least one child, but that's all. Why?" Carrie poured two cups of coffee and handed one to Kelly as she pointed to the cream and sugar.

"I met her today." Kelly spooned sugar and creamer into her cup. "She's staying with Elise for a few weeks. I have to say she seems...well...a little odd."

"What kind of odd?" Carrie took her mug to the small round table near the window and sat, motioning for Kelly to join her.

Kelly sat in the other chair at the table and took a sip of her coffee. "She just stood there and stared at me when I first saw her. She talked to her aunt, but didn't have anything to say to me as we were introduced...not even a 'nice to meet you.' Seriously, I thought at first maybe there was something wrong with her. Then again, maybe she's shy. I guess we'll see. One thing's for sure, she's nothing like her aunt."

"I've heard her talk about her niece. She's very close to her, but she's never brought her into the office. What does she look like?"

"Pretty. Okay, very pretty. She might even be beautiful if she'd smile. But I didn't see her do that, so I don't know." Kelly shrugged.

"You must've noticed more than that." Carrie held her mug in both hands and leaned forward, her elbows on the table. "Come on, give."

"All right. Let me think." Kelly stared off into space. "Hair blonde, shoulder length. Eyes brown. About five-six. Nice legs. How's that?" Kelly grinned and took another sip from her coffee.

"Oh, come on. Well, it should be interesting working for Elise, anyway. I like her, plus she's a bit of a character. She's always entertaining."

"A bit of a character. That's for sure." Kelly laughed. "She was trimming the palm trees in her front yard when I got there today. I mistook her for the gardener."

"That's Elise, all right. I can tell you this, there's one thing you won't have to worry about, and that's getting paid. She always pays on time. In fact, she's been known to give our workers a little extra under the table for doing a great job. We're not supposed to know, but we don't mind."

"Hmm...well, it's nice to know I won't have to remind her to pay me, anyway." Kelly took another sip of her coffee. "That goes a long way in my book."

Chapter Three

KELLY PULLED INTO ELISE'S driveway and noticed a metallic blue Mercedes SLK350 sitting in the driveway over by the garage. A convertible, the hard top was up. She wondered if it was Elise's or Andrea's or if they had a visitor. Either way, she gave it a good looking over. She had no idea what they cost but she knew it was way more than her Dodge Durango.

Elise met her at the door and after a short trip to the kitchen for some sweet tea, they settled in the office to talk. Elise spread Kelly's drawings on her desk. "It's much easier to visualize your design in here." She looked down at the design, then at the wall. She held the drawing up at arm's length. She nodded. "This will definitely do. I love it."

"If you're happy, I'm happy. The middle section does stick out from the wall farther than the others, but it gives it some depth. That's a lot of bookcase to be a flat design."

"I agree. It adds a whole new dimension to the room. Let's pull the chairs out to where they'll be when the bookcases are finished and make sure the room doesn't look crowded, though."

"Sure, we can do that." Kelly moved the chairs away from the wall, took out her measuring tape, and moved the chairs to where they would sit after the bookcases were installed. For reference, she put the open measuring tape on the floor to show where the front of the bookcase would be. "How's that?"

Before Elise could answer, Andrea showed up at the door. Kelly found herself trying not to stare at Andrea. *Is this the same woman? She seems almost childlike dressed in that T-shirt and shorts. The ponytail and no makeup add to that impression, but she's definitely no child.*

This time Andrea only glanced at her aunt, then looked right at Kelly when she came in. "I'm sorry to interrupt, but could I borrow my aunt for a minute?" Andrea's voice was soft and nearly musical.

"Uh, sure." Kelly wasn't ready for the immediate reaction she felt to hearing Andrea speak to her. The tingle spread from her brain to several other parts of her right away. She mentally slapped herself. She wasn't going to be smitten with Andrea. Not a good idea.

Elise followed Andrea from the room, leaving Kelly to get her breathing back to normal. *This can't be happening. I am not going to fall for some beautiful rich girl. No. No. No. Just because she isn't the snob she seemed to be last time doesn't mean I should let myself drown in those big brown eyes. Oh no.* She sat down in one of the chairs she had moved. She willed herself to take a deep breath and think about bookcases.

A couple of minutes later, Elise slid into the chair across from Kelly. "I apologize for that interruption."

"No problem, now, where were we? Oh yes, the chairs. How does this feel, space-wise?"

Elise looked around from her seat. "It looks perfect from here. Plenty of room."

"All right, then, how about the doors on the cabinets? Would you like the doors to be solid wood or would you prefer wood with glass panes or plain glass?"

"You know, the wood doors with glass inserts sound good to me. Plain glass doors would look a little too stark. Solid wood doors seem a bit too heavy. I'd like to keep the look in here light, even with all those books that will be in here."

"To tell you the truth, I like that design the best, too, but I would've given you what you wanted if you liked one of the other designs better. They're your cabinets, after all."

Elise smiled. "I can see that you have a great design sense. Carrie told me about the rocking chair you made her from the wood from her grandfather's tree and showed me a picture of it. That says you not only have a good eye, but also a good heart. A feel for what's good and what will mean something to someone."

Kelly smiled and looked down at the designs, and back at Elise. "That was something special I made Carrie. She's a good friend

Elise reached over and patted Kelly's arm. "You know, I like you, Kelly. I know good people when I see them and you're good people."

"Thank you. Now please don't take this the wrong way, but you seem a lot more Floridian than New Yorker to me. Have you spent a lot of time here?"

"It shows, doesn't it? My grandparents and parents wintered here and I spent every bit of time with them I could. I've had a second home here for a long time now because I love being here in Fort Myers."

"It shows that you care about this place very much. It's gorgeous.

I'm glad you enjoy it here."

"And I'm going to like working with you. How soon can we get started on my new bookcases?"

"I should be able to start on it next week. I can build part of it elsewhere and install it in sections, all at the same time, if that's satisfactory. Do you want the back of the bookcases open to the wall and installed permanently or do you want them as stand-alone units that could be moved?"

"I want them to be a permanent part of the house. Also, I'd like the color of the wall behind to show through the open shelves. So, let's attach them to the wall."

"All right. I'll get started on it right away. I'll call you once I have the design ready for you to approve. Does that work for you?"

"Works for me. Now, how about you stay for lunch with us? Andrea's putting together something tasty in there and I'm sure there's plenty. Besides, it'd be good for her to see the face of someone her own age for a change, not just mine."

"I don't want to intrude."

Elise gave a reassuring touch to Kelly's arm. "Not at all. So how about it? Oh, I'm sorry. I should've asked you whether you need to be somewhere else."

"Actually, I don't. I'd love to, thank you."

Elise and Kelly strolled out to the lanai. Andrea beckoned them to sit at the small glass-topped white wicker table.

"How long do you think it will take you to build and install the bookcases?" Andrea asked.

"A few weeks. I'll have them finished before Elise needs to go back to New York for Thanksgiving and Christmas." Kelly took a sip of her tea. "So, do you live in New York, too?"

"I used to. Not now." Andrea abruptly stood and strode toward the kitchen door. "Lunch is almost ready. Be right back." She disappeared into the kitchen.

"I'm sorry, did I say something wrong?"

Elise reached over and patted Kelly's hand. "No, sweetie, you didn't. She's sensitive right now. Look, she just went through a nasty breakup and being here with me is therapeutic for her. I think she simply needs to feel her feet under her again."

"I'm so sorry. I shouldn't stay..." Kelly started to get up, but Elise stopped her with a hand on her shoulder.

"No. Stay. Don't worry, she'll be all right and you didn't say or do anything wrong. She might sound a little gruff, but she's such a softie inside. She's still hurting. That she said anything at all to you is something good. She didn't come out of her room much for several days after she got here. At least now she's gotten herself a rental car and run to the grocery a couple of times. I'm pretty sure she's even driven out to Sanibel or Fort Myers Beach once or twice. So, she's getting better."

"Well, that's good. I know how it feels to go through a breakup and it's not fun. Sometimes what you need most is someone to talk to, to let it all out. You must be that person for Andrea."

Elise nodded as she smiled. "She's always come to me, even when she was little. Her mother died when she was very young, after giving birth prematurely to her little brother. Shortly after that, her brother died, poor little guy. Her father, my brother, was never the same after that. Andrea got the short stick."

"Wow, that's awful," Kelly said, her eyes wandering toward the door to the kitchen. "She's been through a lot, hasn't she?"

"She has, but she's a strong one, that girl. She just needs some time. I'm starting to wonder if she actually wants to go back to New York, since she seems much more relaxed here. Well, time will tell, that's for sure."

Just then, the kitchen door swung open and Andrea emerged, bearing a tray with ham sandwiches. Kelly jumped up to help, taking the tray to place it on the table.

"Thanks, Kelly. That was nice of you. I'll be right back with the iced tea pitcher and the rest."

"Please, let me help. I do know my way around a kitchen." Kelly smiled.

"Okay, you can carry the tea pitcher out for me." Andrea turned without smiling back. Once they were in the kitchen alone, Andrea made a sudden turn to face Kelly. "Look, I hope my aunt isn't trying to set us up or something. I'm definitely not looking for a date or anything, but my aunt sometimes…"

"Excuse me? I don't think that's what I'm here for. I'm here to build her some bookcases and cabinets."

"Right. Like she needs them." Andrea leaned back against the kitchen counter, crossed her arms, and stared at Kelly.

"Actually, she told me she's planning to make this her year-round home soon and wants to move her books here. Do you think she's thinking something else? I mean, the construction company referred me. There was no way she could've known…"

"That's true. All right, it's possible I overreacted." Andrea unfolded her arms. "She does like to play matchmaker, though. She also believes she knows best. And...she's probably wondering what's keeping us in here." She picked up the napkins, forks, and plates, and headed for the door to the lanai.

"If she's trying to matchmake us, it's not going to work. You don't even live here. We should get back out there before she starts to wonder what's taking so long." Kelly picked up the tea pitcher and followed.

"Good plan. Besides, you aren't even my type," Andrea said over her shoulder as she pushed open the door.

What? Her type? And what makes her think she could be my type? Maybe I'm not attracted to gorgeous blondes with big brown eyes.

Chapter Four

"ASTONISHINGLY ENOUGH, I'M RATHER attracted to her," Kelly told Shawn and Carrie as they sat down to supper a couple of nights later. She'd told them the story about meeting Andrea and what Andrea had said to her while Carrie settled Piper with some roast beef.

"She said I'm not her type and I told her she doesn't even live here, so I wasn't interested, either."

"Well, how much are you going to have to see her? I mean, other than when you're installing the bookcases. You can do most of the work elsewhere, right?" Shawn asked.

"True, I don't have to see her that much. That might squash Elise's matchmaking ideas, if that's what's going on. I didn't see it, but Andrea believed it was. As I said, I am attracted to her. She's beautiful, but she's also coming out of a horrible breakup from what Elise said. Besides, Andrea made it clear she isn't interested in anyone, especially someone who's not her type, as she put it."

"How attracted to her are you? I mean, is she simply pretty to look at or...what?"

"Confession? I was mesmerized by her voice. She's gorgeous. I don't know. It seems like a dead-end street, though. She's only here for a while to recuperate. I don't know where she lives now, but it's not here. When I asked her if she lived in New York like Elise, she pretty much said 'not now' and got up and left the room."

"Oh well, she sounds like she's hurting and wouldn't be interested in anyone right now. That's totally understandable. Hmm...I wonder if she meant she doesn't live there now, or she didn't want to answer that question right now."

"I hadn't considered all of that," Kelly said. "I figured she was just blowing me off. I was sure I'd said something to upset her, but Elise told me I hadn't and that it was okay."

"You're very easy to talk to. Maybe she needs a friend while she's here. You could hang out together if she likes and let it go at that," Carrie said.

Kelly nodded. "Good idea. That might keep Elise happy. Besides, if I let Andrea know that my interest is to get to know her as a friend, she might relax a little. That might be good for her while she's here. Anyway, if Elise can see we're playing nice, at least she won't try setting her up with someone else. That is, of course, unless Andrea wants to be set up."

"What do you mean?" Shawn put her fork down and looked up at Kelly.

"Maybe she wouldn't mind being set up with someone but not me."

"Kelly..." Shawn picked up her fork and pointed it at her. "Are you honestly thinking that?"

"She's made it very clear that I'm not her type. It could be that she'd rather hang out with some more urbane women. Or she could be one of those women who likes the more feminine types." She stared at her biscuit as she pushed the butter across it with her knife. "Or maybe she wouldn't be caught dead with one of the 'help' around here."

"If she really is like that, she isn't worthy of your interest no matter how pretty she is or what her voice makes you feel," Carrie said. "But maybe, just maybe, she's exactly what she looks like...someone who's hurting. If that's what's happening, she doesn't need a date right now. She needs a friend. You're very good at being a friend, Kelly."

Kelly let out a sigh. "Yes, I'm good at being a friend." She sighed again. "One of these days, however, I'd like to be good at being a partner. I want a relationship like you two have. But on the other hand, I can't make something out of nothing. There has to be something there, something from both of us, to make it work." Kelly picked at her green beans.

"You don't think there could be?" Carrie asked.

"To tell you the truth, we've scarcely gotten to know each other. I felt something...like she was definitely interested, too. I could see something in her eyes."

"If you are too, I'd say you need to back up and think about this," Carrie said. "Give things a chance to see if something develops. Don't write her off yet as just another snobby rich girl."

"I need to go back again and re-measure after I show Elise the drawings I have. If Andrea's there, she might be interested in something very low key and a chance to talk."

"There you go. I've got a feeling she might appreciate having that right now more than anything else."

Shawn chimed in, "I do feel for her. It's hard getting back up after having your heart broken in tiny pieces. It takes time to put it back together and I can't imagine her being able to do that during a short vacation. Didn't you say she's staying with her aunt for a few weeks?"

"Right, that's what Elise said, although she also made it clear Andrea could stay as long as she wants."

"Never know what will happen, do you? I wonder if she could be working from her aunt's, telecommuting," Shawn suggested. "She must've had a job of some kind wherever she came from."

"A pretty good one, too, if you ask me," Kelly said. "She's driving a rental car, but it's no Chevy. It's a Mercedes. Unless she's independently wealthy, she's got a good career going of some kind."

"So, you ask her what she does for a living and you can talk about that unless she truly doesn't want to talk to you." Carrie got up and retrieved the ice tea pitcher.

"I guess so. It's possible she doesn't trust me to not be nosy. Who knows? It's possible she could use a pretty good listener closer to her own age. I'm good at that."

"Yes, you are. You're an excellent listener, as a matter of fact." Carrie smiled at her as she refilled her glass. "I can give you a reference if you need one."

Kelly grinned back at her. "Thanks. I might take you up on that."

Shawn reached for another biscuit. "Look, Kelly, you're a great friend and she'd be lucky to have you in her life. If she isn't in a space to have someone to talk to, it's on her. All you can do is offer."

"Thanks, guys. When I go back over to show Elise my drawings I'll try to talk to Andrea. I'm sure she could use someone to talk to while she's here, if nothing else."

Chapter Five

KELLY PULLED INTO ELISE'S driveway two days later with the drawings and the Mercedes gone. *So much for getting a chance to talk to Andrea today. Since Elise knew I was coming, so did Andrea. Maybe she doesn't want to see me. Yeah, that was possible after our last conversation. Well, I guess that's pretty much that.*

Kelly couldn't hide her surprise when Andrea answered the door. The slight smile on Andrea's face made her look much more pleasant than the last time.

"Well, hi." Kelly answered Andrea's smile with one of her own.

"Hi, yourself. Guess you're surprised to see me, right?" Andrea motioned for Kelly to come in. "Aunt Elise had another appointment this morning, after all, and she said that since I knew what she wanted, I should meet with you."

"If she's happy with you approving the drawings, I am, too." Kelly stepped into the entry hall. "I admit I'm surprised to see you because the Mercedes is gone. I assumed it was yours, so I also assumed you'd be in it."

"It is mine. Actually, it's my rental. But when she asked if she could borrow it, of course I said yes. I almost never say no to Aunt Elise."

"I can imagine most people don't say no to her." Kelly grinned. "She's one of those people."

"No, they don't. Not because she's mean or anything, but because people usually want to say yes. It's always been that way. So, can I get you something to drink…some iced tea or water or a soda?"

"Sure, some iced tea would be nice. We could spread the drawings out on the kitchen counter, if you like."

"Works for me. That big island in the kitchen is great for that kind of stuff."

Kelly followed Andrea into the kitchen, taking in the lovely view of Andrea's backside and bare legs.

"I'll get us some tea while we look at the plans. I promise not to spill anything on them." Andrea turned to retrieve two ice tea glasses waiting on the counter near the refrigerator.

"Thanks, I appreciate that." Kelly spread the drawings on the highly polished, light grey granite counter in the center of the kitchen. She was running her hand along the ogee bullnose and around the corner as Andrea returned with two glasses of iced tea. "This is a very nice countertop."

Andrea set the glasses away from Kelly's sketches. "Aunt Elise wasn't sure she'd like granite countertops. But when the contractor showed her all the different choices for the edges and colors, she was sold. She didn't want the usual rounded edges. It came out nicely, didn't it?"

"Very nice. Whoever did this, I admire their workmanship."

"I guess you don't know that the company that referred you built this house. Everything in it, they did. You're the first outside contractor that's ever been allowed to work on anything in this place. Obviously, they trust you."

"Well, I'm close with someone who works there, but they've seen my work, too." Kelly took a sip of her tea. "Good tea. Thanks." She put the glass back down away from the sketches. "Anyway, how about we take a look at the plans?"

"Glad you like the tea. Okay, walk me through it," Andrea said, leaning over the counter to look.

"These shelves are open to the wall behind." Kelly pointed to the sketches. "Elise said she wanted the wall color to show through the open shelves on the top. The bottom cabinets are also open to the back, but they have doors on them. Even though there's glass in them, they'll still give the lower sections a cleaner appearance. She and I thought that might look better since there'll be chairs in front of them."

"They look like they'd be perfect in there. They have the same basic style as her desk and chairs. What color will they be?"

"She said she wanted them painted or stained white. I'm going to give her a couple of samples when we're ready and she can decide on the final finish then. A good coat of acrylic should make them durable and clean easily." Kelly looked at Andrea. "You like the look of them?"

Andrea ran a finger over the drawings, as if she was trying to feel the texture of the wood. "I'm sure Aunt Elise will love these. When do you think you'll start working on them?" Her voice almost a whisper.

"Now that the drawings are approved, I'll go buy the wood and get started on it this afternoon or tomorrow, depending on what I can get this afternoon."

"How long will it be before you come back again to start working in the house?"

"Two to three weeks, if all goes as planned. Are you still going to be here?"

"Maybe. I'm not sure how long I'll be staying. Aunt Elise said I'm welcome to stay as long as I want, but..."

"But..."

Andrea sighed, then looked up at Kelly. "If you're not in a hurry to leave, bring your tea and let's sit in the dinette for a little bit."

"Actually, I'm in no hurry at all. I'd be happy to chat with you for a while."

Taken aback at Andrea's change in demeanor from the previous visit, Kelly rolled up the drawings but left them on the counter. She picked up her tea and followed Andrea to the little built-in dinette in the corner of the kitchen. Once they'd settled onto a bench, they took a sip of their tea in silence. Kelly waited for Andrea to say something else, but when she didn't, Kelly broke the stillness.

"What do you have to go back home to? Or do you need to be back there for your job?"

Andrea raised her eyes to look at Kelly. Those gorgeous brown eyes, with their long eyelashes made Kelly take a deep breath. She tried to mask it by looking down at her tea for a second.

"I don't have a regular job to go back to, no. I was with a very wealthy woman who didn't want me to work at a regular job of any kind because it interfered with her travel and party plans. I was working at an art gallery before we met, but cut back my hours because she insisted. I thought it was fun in the beginning, not working full-time. To tell you the truth, though, working part-time got old fast for me."

Andrea pushed her already sweating glass around in its little puddle. Kelly watched her and waited. After nearly a minute of silence, Andrea took a deep breath and looked up at Kelly.

"I finally opened a gallery of my own in SoHo and started spending more time there. But again, I tried to please Jo by working only a few days each week and just had the gallery open part-time. I was in love and believed it would all work out. It didn't. Short story, she found someone more fun than I am who was willing to be arm candy—a kept playmate. Oh, and the new one is in her twenties instead of nearly forty. I keep thinking she'll tire of her, but so far, she hasn't. Stupid tale, but true."

Kelly wanted to reach over and touch Andrea's hand, but didn't.

"It's not stupid at all. You loved her. You probably would've done anything she asked." Kelly shook her head slowly. "I have a friend who let herself become something she wasn't because she was in love. It didn't last either. You have to be yourself."

"I know that now. The trouble is, I'm not sure who I am any more or what I want to do. I'm not broke or anything. I have the gallery and I can make it on my own." She took a deep breath. "On the other hand, I can't sit around and do nothing about this situation."

"No, you can't do that, but right now you're still hurting. Sometimes you need time to let yourself heal. The right thing will come to you in its own good time." Kelly stared at her tea, and pushed her glass around for a few seconds in its own little puddle. She looked back up at Andrea. "Look, if you need a friend, I'm here. If you want to get out of the house for a few hours and do something, I'm here. No strings, simply one friend with another." She reached into her pocket and took out a case with her business cards in it. She handed one of the cards to Andrea. "Here's my cell number. Don't hesitate to call me if you just want to talk, okay?"

"Thanks, Kelly. I'm sorry if I was a little cold to you earlier. I thought I didn't want to be around anyone but Aunt Elise. It wasn't personal, please believe me." Andrea looked at the business card, and back at Kelly. "You seem like a very nice person and I'd like to be friends. I appreciate it."

Kelly shook her head and let out a little laugh. "So, do you think Elise threw us together today hoping this might happen?"

"I wouldn't put it past her." Andrea grinned a tiny grin. "She's such a wonderful woman and I'm proud to call her my aunt, but she's more like a mom to me."

"Well, now you also have a friend here. How's that?" Kelly once again felt the urge to reach over and hold Andrea's hand, but she pushed it down.

"Thanks, I do appreciate that. Do you have another one of those cards?"

"Sure." Kelly reached into her pocket and into the case for another card as Andrea walked across the kitchen to a little desk in the corner, bringing back a pen. Andrea wrote something on the back of the card and handed it back to Kelly. Andrea had written a phone number on the back, along with her name.

"It's my cell. This friendship thing goes both ways. You can call me, too, if you'd like to have someone to go to dinner with or something."

She stopped suddenly. "I'm sorry, I didn't even ask you if you were in a relationship or something. I wouldn't want to intrude..."

Kelly laughed. "Nope, I'm not in a relationship or even dating anyone right now. You wouldn't be intruding on anything, believe me. You can call me any time."

"Oh, good. Well, I guess I'd better let you get on with my aunt's bookcases. Thanks for letting me bend your ear. Feel free to call me any time, too. I've pretty much been hanging around the house here and I'm sure my aunt would like to see me out doing something or at least talking to someone else besides her."

Kelly got up and headed to the sink to rinse out her glass. "I do need to take one more set of measurements. I like to double check everything before I start cutting. Would it be okay to do it now?" She turned from the sink and began gathering her drawings.

"No problem. I'll show you in there and leave you alone to do your thing. I don't want to bother you."

As they walked down the hall to the office, Kelly said, "Believe me, you'd be no bother at all. If you've got something else to do, it's fine. It won't take me long."

Andrea opened the doors to the office. "If it's all right with you, I'll stick around and watch."

They pulled the chairs farther away from the wall and Kelly showed her where they'd be after the bookcases were in. "This is what the room will look like, if you can imagine the wall full of shelves and cabinets. Still like it?"

Andrea sat down at the desk, in working position. "I do like it and I'm sure Aunt Elise will, too. This room's certainly large enough to carry that off."

"Good. Glad you agree." Kelly stood back and looked at the space again. "I have an idea. The three bookcases in the middle should include doors on the bottom as I drew them. But what do you think about having the end sections with open shelves all the way to the bottom? There's room."

"That sounds great to me, but I think we should ask her."

"Want to ask her when she gets home and have her call me? Or you can call me. Whichever. But I'd like to give her a choice. There's an extra copy of the drawings in the truck that I can give you to show her. You can explain her options and she can decide. She'll be back this afternoon, right?"

"Yes, she will. I'll make sure she sees this when she gets in and I'll explain the open shelf option. If she has any questions, we can call you. How about that?"

"You got it. I can go for the wood as soon as she's happy with this. I know she said to let you decide, but…"

Andrea nodded. "I know, I'd like her to have the final say as well. She should make that decision regarding the cabinets on the end, too. It's her office, after all."

"It is and she'll be the one that will look at them every time she's in there."

"I'm glad you see it the same way. Now she has a choice…options, if you will. Let me double-check these measurements, and I'll be out of your way." Kelly grinned as she reached into a pocket of her shorts for her tape measure.

Andrea grinned back. "Thanks, but you're not in my way at all. Here, let me help hold the end of the tape measure, at least."

.

Chapter Six

SHORTLY AFTER LUNCH, KELLY'S phone went off. She sat down in the kitchen dinette nook to take the call. Piper jumped up to sit right next to her.

Without even a hello, Elise started right in. "Kelly, I love your design for my bookcases." Kelly could hear the smile in her voice. "Thanks for offering me a second option. Andrea agrees with me that either of them works in this space."

Kelly felt herself grinning. "You're welcome. I'm glad you like it." She reached over to scratch Piper's ears, which always made Piper lean into Kelly's side even more.

"Since I do have tons of books, let's go with your second idea of having doors on the bottom halves of the three in the middle, with shelves all the way down on the end cabinets."

"Great. Thanks for calling right away. I'll get right on it," Kelly said. "One more question. Do you want hardware on the doors? I mean, handles to open them. Or would you rather have them with a slot cut into the top of each door to pull them open?"

"You're full of options, aren't you? I hadn't considered that. Tell you what, let me mull that over for a little while and let you know. I'll take a look at the drawer pulls and the like on my desk and other things in the room to help me decide. Can I get back to you in a couple of days about that?"

"Of course, you can. There's no rush, since I don't have to know until I'm building the cabinet doors. Take your time." Kelly had stopped scratching Piper's ears, so Piper began patting Kelly's arm with her paw. Kelly grinned at her, then resumed her ear scratching with her free hand.

"And if I decide on door handles, we can make a decision about them later. If we do put on handles, I'd like them to look as much like my desk and other things as possible but you already know that."

Kelly grinned again. "I kind of figured that'd be what you wanted. We can do that. There are lots of options, as well as plenty of places to order them if we can't find something you like at one of the local stores. We'd only need three of them, so it wouldn't make any difference in the price, one way or another. Let me know as soon as you decide."

"I will," Elise said. "Oh, by the way, Andrea told me you two had a pleasant chat."

"She offered me some iced tea and we sat and talked for a few minutes. I enjoyed her company."

"She also said that she thought you were very nice. I guess that means you two are getting along well?"

"She did help me re-measure, which was handy. So yes, I guess you could say we're getting along well. You have a lovely niece." Kelly decided she didn't need to mention that they were planning to get together sometime. She figured that'd be up to Andrea.

Kelly heard Elise release a small sigh. "She means the world to me. She doesn't know anyone here her own age. I didn't mean to be presumptuous, but I kind of hoped you two would hit it off, friend-wise. She seems so lonely. Anyway, I'll let you know about the doors as soon as I can. And thanks for a great design. I'm sure it's going to look great."

"You're welcome. I'll get right on it."

Kelly was about ready to end the call, when she heard Elise say something in a near whisper. "And thanks for being kind to Andrea."

"Elise, that's easy. She's a very pleasant person to be around, just like her aunt."

Kelly hit end on the call. *Yes, Andrea's a pleasure for sure.* She reached into her pocket and found the card with Andrea's number on it and took it out to look at it. She ran her thumb across the card, feeling the indentation of the numbers. Piper reached up to smell the card before lying down on the bench, apparently deciding it was of no interest. Kelly decided to wait a day before calling Andrea. Or not. She wasn't sure what to do.

Andrea seemed to be asking her to call her. Maybe she'd like to go somewhere, have coffee or something, and chat. She decided she'd think about this for a bit first. She was startled out of her deliberation by her phone. The phone ID showing it was Shawn.

"Hey, bud. We were wondering if you'd like to come over for supper tonight. I know you were just here a few days ago, but Carrie's making one of your favorites and there's always much more than we can eat. Piper can help eat some of it, too, as usual. Of course, if you've other plans..."

"No, I don't have other plans, actually. Every single thing she makes is one of my favorites. Which one is it this time?"

"How about country fried steak?"

"Oh yeah, that sounds great and I'd love to. About six, as usual?"

"Yep, the usual. We're looking forward to seeing you. Oh, and get ready to take home some leftovers. For some reason, she always thinks you can't take care of yourself and you need someone to feed the two of you." Shawn laughed. "Of course, if it came down to it, Piper would eat kibble. I doubt if you'd want to do that."

"Yeah, well, I guess I do eat out a lot. I sure do like Carrie's cooking, but you know I can cook when I want to."

"Look, you know that and I know that, but Carrie…, she's convinced you need a good woman in your life to take care of you." Shawn chuckled again. "I did. She's absolutely convinced you do, too."

"Maybe I do. But unlike you, the right woman has not yet taken a flying leap into my arms or moved in down the street."

"Give it time, my friend. I'm sure yours is on her way and you don't know it yet. We'll see you at supper tonight."

Chapter Seven

KELLY'S TIRES CRUNCHED ON Shawn's crushed-shell driveway as she pulled into her home away from home. She always enjoyed time spent with Shawn and Carrie. She and Shawn had been friends since grade school and she'd been 'best woman' at their wedding last year. The little Florida cracker house Shawn had renovated before they were married still had the same appeal it always had, but it was now a warm, inviting home with the addition of Carrie's touches.

As Kelly walked up to the screened-in porch, she thought about all the hours she and Shawn had spent out there, bare feet up on the porch railing, lifting a few and solving the problems of the world—including their own. Not to mention talking about Carrie before she and Shawn finally got together. They both had affections for Carrie, but Carrie only had eyes for Shawn from the day they met and Kelly knew those two were meant for each other.

Before she could knock, Shawn opened the door and grabbed her into a hug. Piper ran for Carrie, who was close behind with a hug for her as well as a kiss on her cheek before she scooped up the little dog. Yep, other than her own house, this was the next best thing to home she had and she loved it. She loved them. It was obvious that Piper loved them, too.

"Come on, Piper," Carrie said as she carried the little dog to the kitchen. "Let's get you something good to eat." Piper looked like she was smiling as she looked over Carrie's shoulder at Kelly as if to say, "Look, Mom! I'm getting my dinner first!"

A few minutes later, the humans were sitting down to one of Carrie's home-cooked meals of country fried steak, mashed potatoes and gravy, and green beans. Of course, there were hot biscuits with butter and for Kelly, Carrie always put out grape jelly.

"Didn't you go back over to Elise's today?" Carrie asked as she handed Kelly a plate loaded with the flaky golden biscuits.

"Yes, I did. Today was to show her the drawings and give her the chance to suggest changes and approve them." With the tips of her fingers, Kelly removed two of the still hot biscuits from the basket. She blew on her fingers to cool them after she dropped the biscuits onto her plate. "But guess what, she was a no-show. She had Andrea look at them instead and approve them."

"Andrea? Really? That's odd." Carrie paused, her head cocked to one side in thought. "Elise is quite particular about her projects. I'm surprised she didn't want to look at the plans herself."

"I thought so, too. Not that I minded spending some one-on-one time with Andrea, but it did seem rather odd. This project isn't in the guest room. It's in Elise's office."

"Hmm...even more reason to want to see what you came up with before you started on them. Very odd."

"And even more odd was that she asked Andrea to borrow her car. So even if Andrea wanted to go somewhere, she was pretty much stuck with me. It was almost like she was trying to throw us together. I'll have to admit it wasn't in the least unpleasant." Kelly grinned. "She's gorgeous."

"Well, then, I can see what you mean regarding feeling no pain about it." Shawn tried not to laugh. "I'm sure your snowbird customer's very nice, but I bet her niece is a whole lot cuter."

Kelly had picked up her fork to begin eating, but instead twirled it around slowly in her fingers before laying it on her plate. "It's not like that, actually."

"Are you sure? Sure, sounds like a classic set up to me," Shawn said.

"I know what it looks like, but I've realized something. Carrie, as you suspected, Andrea needs a friend right now and I told her I'd be just that. Look, she isn't planning to stay, I'm sure, and there's no future in getting involved with someone that won't be around. We exchanged phone numbers and we might go out sometime...not as dates, as friends only."

"Okay, we got it." Shawn Carrie gave each other looks that said otherwise.

"Stop it, you two. I saw that." Kelly retrieved her fork. "Besides, I came up with another option for the bookcases from what I originally discussed with Elise and asked Andrea to have Elise let me know what she thinks of it. This other option didn't require new drawings yet, so she wouldn't have any trouble visualizing it. Either way, I'll get Elise to sign off on the final design before I start."

"Sounds like a wise idea," Carrie said. "So...looks like you got to spend a little more time with Andrea."

"True, I did."

"What's this Andrea like?" Shawn asked. "Carrie said you told her she was a blonde and had brown eyes, but that's about it."

"Yes, give. I know you've been around her more now, so what's she actually like?" Carrie asked.

"I'd say she looks a little bit like Elise probably looked when she was younger. Dark blonde hair, eyes the prettiest shade of brown with amber flecks in them I've probably ever seen, and a beautiful smile. She's probably about five feet six. I'd say she has a lovely figure. She's perfect like she is. How's that for a description?"

Shawn and Carrie looked at each other. "You're not falling for her, already are you?"

"Me? No. Why would you say that?" Kelly asked as she buttered a biscuit.

"Why? I don't think I've ever heard you describe a woman quite like that, that's why."

"Can I help it if she's beautiful? She just is. I can admire someone without having a thing for her. Besides, we hardly know each other." She didn't look up as she reached for the grape jelly.

Shawn laughed. "The last time you were here, you seemed rather, shall we say taken with her. Hardly knowing a woman hasn't stopped you in the past for having a thing for her. I only hope you aren't setting yourself up for a big disappointment with someone like that."

"I'm not falling for her. She's simply someone in need of a friend right now. Besides, like I said, she isn't going to be here very much longer and I don't think a long-distance thing would work out, even if we did like each other that way."

Carrie put her hand on Kelly's arm. "I'm sure she appreciates you being kind to her. Everyone can use a friend and I'm sure she's happy you came along when you did. Who knows, it's possible she'll stay in touch after she goes back to wherever she lives. She might come back to visit or you could go visit her. The important thing is, well, I guess we just don't want to see you get hurt."

"Right. Anyway, I'm simply being sociable. That's it. Don't worry about me. But I did think it might be nice to invite her along and the four of us have dinner or something. I think she'd enjoy getting out with other people and I know you'd like her. What do you think?"

"Sure," Shawn said. "If you'd like to ask her out, we could all go somewhere for lunch or dinner and keep it very casual. Hey, we could all go play miniature golf!"

"Really, Shawn? Miniature golf?" Carrie shook her head.

"What's wrong with that? Doesn't it sound like fun? We could get hot dogs and sodas and play a round. It's a great way to get to know someone, chatting while waiting your turn."

"You know what, that does sound like fun," Kelly said. "I'll see if she wants to go and I'll get back to you. But don't be disappointed if she'd rather not. Believe it or not, there are people out there who don't like miniature golf. But in case that happens, the same place has those little race cars you can drive, too. And batting cages. There should be something she likes, I'd think."

"I'm sorry I was giving you a hard time about this, Kelly," Carrie said. "It does sound like fun. Give us a heads up if or when you want to go somewhere together. If that doesn't seem like her thing, I'd be glad to make dinner here for us. I'd even make a chocolate pie..." She grinned, waggling her eyebrows and making Shawn and Kelly laugh.

"I'm thinking even if she decides not to go, we can still do it. The three of us have lots of fun there. But I'm good with dinner here, too," Shawn said. "You do seem to like her and if you like her, I'm sure we'll like her, too."

Chapter Eight

KELLY PUNCHED IN ANDREA'S number, her hands shaking. She hesitated before the last number, took a deep breath, erased the potential call, and put the phone in her pocket. She walked out the sliding glass door onto her lanai with Piper trailing along after her, tail wagging as usual.

What if Andrea isn't into ordinary things like miniature golf? What if she's more interested in shopping in fancy places or dinner at upscale restaurants? After all, she is from New York City and drives around in an expensive car, even if it is a rental.

Looking around, she patted herself on the back for all the hard work that had gone into this house. Last year, there had been only a little concrete patio out here, but now there was a comfortable screened and glassed-in lanai big enough to entertain in. It was solely her work for the most part. It hadn't been easy, but it was worth it.

She liked sitting on the lanai in the evenings with Piper. The little dog always wanted to sit in her lap or right next to her with her head in Kelly's lap. That position made it much easier for Kelly to scratch her ears or neck. Kelly had adopted Piper as a pup last year. Piper had rested her head on Kelly's lap the first time she saw her and had come home with her that day. She had scarcely plopped herself down into one of the cushioned chairs when her phone buzzed.

"Andrea! Hi." Kelly couldn't help the smile that instantly lit her face. Piper came running and jumped up in her lap for her usual ear scratching.

"Hi, yourself, and I think it's about time you called me Andi. My friends do and I think we can call ourselves friends now, right?"

"Of course, Andi. What's up?" Kelly's grin was even wider, if that was possible, as she absently stroked Piper's neck.

"Well, I was just sitting here doing nothing and wondering if you were sitting there doing nothing, too."

"I'd say that pretty much describes what I'm doing right now. Almost, anyway." Kelly fiddled with the seashell sitting on the side table. "Were you thinking about doing something?"

"Well, yes. Nothing big. How about going out for a drink somewhere? I was thinking it would be fun to be out for a bit."

"I think I could manage that. Where would you like to go?" Kelly absently ran her fingers over the smooth inside of the seashell.

"I'm open. It could be a restaurant that has a bar, or just a bar. Either's fine with me. I'd assume by now you've eaten supper, right?"

"Yes, I have. Have you eaten?"

"I ate something earlier. I have an idea. Would you rather go somewhere for some dessert and coffee?" Andi asked.

"That sounds even better to me. How about we meet at the Perkins over on Cleveland Avenue? It's about halfway between us and they make great pie and other kinds of desserts as well. How does that sound to you?" Kelly sat up on the chair and moved the shell back to its home.

"That's great. I've heard their bakery's excellent. At least their ads on TV look good. Meet you there in, say, twenty minutes, if that's good with you?"

"Perfect. See you there." Kelly hit end on her phone and sat back in the chair for a few seconds, smiling. She picked Piper up and gave her a hug as her face was being licked before putting her down. She jumped up and headed for her keys.

Fifteen minutes later she pulled into the parking lot at Perkins Restaurant. This time of the evening and on a weeknight Kelly knew it wouldn't be crowded—even during snowbird season—and it wasn't. Snowbirds were famous for showing up for the early bird specials, which ended by five. She scanned the parking lot for Andi's Mercedes, and not seeing it, she decided to get out and wait by the door

A familiar voice behind Kelly startled her out of her thoughts. It was her on and off friend and former sort-of-girlfriend, Tracy, with her latest conquest. She didn't think Tracy noticed her at first, being busy hanging onto the arm of the tall, handsome woman she was with. But she did see her as they were almost ready to walk in the door.

"Well, hi there, Kelly. Great to see you again. It's been awhile. How are you?" Tracy ran her fingers through her long auburn curls, southern belle written all over her. "Waiting for someone, sugar?"

"A friend," Kelly said. "I sure wouldn't want to hold you guys up."

Tracy smiled. "Don't worry, you aren't. Oh, by the way, this is Reagan." She looked up at her date, smiling sweetly. "Reagan, honey, this is my friend, Kelly."

Kelly put out her hand to shake hands and Reagan extricated her hand from Tracy's to do the same, eyeing Kelly but smiling.

"Nice to meet you," they said at the same time.

"You two enjoy your evening," Kelly said. All she wanted to do was get them to move on. Andi would be there any minute now.

"You, too." Tracy tried to reclaim Reagan's hand, but Reagan reached for the door instead and in seconds they were out of sight.

"Friends of yours?" Andi said from behind her as the door closed behind Tracy and Reagan.

Kelly turned quickly and grinned. "One of them. The redhead. The other one's her flavor of the month." Kelly shook her head. "Water under the bridge. How about some pie? It's my treat."

Andi grinned back. "Thanks, I'm in."

They opened the door into the bakery, which took up the front section of Perkins Restaurant. The sweet, fruity pie aromas were mouth-watering as they made their way to the hostess to be seated. Kelly had to stop on the way to gaze at the display case with nearly every kind of pie on their menu, along with several varieties of chocolate chip cookies, just sitting there waiting to be admired and hopefully taken home. Out of habit, she scanned the case for her favorite strawberry pie, even though she knew it was out of season.

Kelly felt herself relax once they slid into a booth with Tracy and Reagan nowhere in sight. She knew Tracy would make a big deal out of anything she thought she might've seen, and later she'd call her and ask all kinds of questions about Andi, as well.

"I didn't see you drive up," Kelly said.

"Oh, I changed cars. I decided to ditch the Mercedes and get something I'd enjoy driving more and worry about less. I got...don't laugh...a Camry."

"Really? As you can see, I'm not laughing. What made you decide to change cars?"

"It's pretty comfortable and I don't have to worry as much about where I park it. I found myself worrying constantly driving that rental Mercedes and parking it in the mall parking lot or at the beach. I was afraid it was going to get door dings and I was going to get charged with it when I turned it in."

"You're planning to be here for a while?"

"I'm going to be here for a while, yes. I'm not quite sure how long, but for long enough to change cars. I blend in more here in it. I liked that Mercedes, but to tell you the truth, it was more what I was expected to drive than what I actually wanted."

"Well, you'll feel more comfortable in that Camry than the Mercedes." Kelly pulled the dessert menus out of the table holder and handed one to Andi.

"I already do. It's easy and fun to drive and I like it. Now, on to some dessert?"

"Oh yeah...this place has a great menu of sweets, especially pie. All kinds of pie. What's your favorite?" Kelly asked, looking at the menu.

Andi opened her menu. "Hmm...I think chocolate is my favorite. How about you?"

"Chocolate pie, huh? My friend Carrie makes the world's best chocolate pie. Just ask her wife, Shawn. Since they got together, it's a wonder Shawn hasn't gained 20 pounds. I love her chocolate pie, too, but I think my all-time favorite's fresh strawberry pie. You know, the one most places only carry part of the year?"

"Oh yes, I know that pie well. I'd say that runs a close second to chocolate pie, for me." Andi continued her scan of the menu. "You have actual friends, huh?" Andi peeked over the menu. Kelly looked up to find Andi grinning from ear to ear. "You know I'm kidding, right?"

"Yes, I do have actual friends. And yes, I do know you're kidding." Kelly grinned back. "It's nice to see you having a good time. You have a wonderful smile, by the way. You should wear it more often."

"Why, Kelly, are you flirting with me?" Andi peeked at her over the menu again.

"Um, no. Well, maybe a little bit." Kelly looked directly into Andi's eyes. "I hope that's okay."

"Yes, it's okay. It's very much okay." Andi smiled again and looked back down at the menu.

Kelly felt a little flutter in her stomach. *Oh, no...not falling for this beautiful woman. She'll return to wherever she came from soon and you'll never see her again.*

She made a point of staring at the menu, telling herself she was looking for the strawberry pie that wouldn't be there. She knew it wasn't, but she kept her eyes there for another minute. She decided to settle for lemon meringue. She put the menu down and found Andi looking back at her.

"What?"

Andi grinned at her. "Nothing. You're cute when you get a little flustered."

Kelly felt a flush begin in her cheeks and picked the menu back up to hide behind. "I'm sure I'm not flustered."

"Fine. You're not, then. Maybe you're just cute."

"Now you're giving me a hard time," Kelly put the menu back down and laughed. "Guess that's fair."

The waiter appeared and began removing the two extra place settings on the table. "Ladies, what can I get you today?"

"Chocolate silk pie and coffee for me," Andi said.

"Lemon meringue and I'll have coffee, too." Kelly put her menu back in the table holder.

"I'll be right back with your order," the waiter said, then disappeared.

Andi crossed her arms and leaned over on the table. "So...how did you get into the woodworking business? That isn't a common occupation for a woman."

"My grandfather let me hang out with him when I was little. I was the second oldest grandkid and I loved following him around. He bought me a scaled down set of tools and taught me how to make things."

"That's so sweet. Not every man wants a little girl in his shop. Seems like they're like automotive shops—bastions of masculinity."

"Grandpop was happy I was interested. None of the rest of his grandkids—boys or girls—ever were. He spent time with me and taught me to make stuff. I loved both the time I spent with him and making the things he showed me. He was a wonderful man."

"He sounds like he was. Do you remember the first thing you made with him?" Andi leaned forward, her chin in her hands.

"Of course. I even still have it. He helped me make my own toolbox and my child-sized set of tools that he gave me is still in there." Kelly smiled absently. "Sometimes I pull it out to look at it and feel close to him again. It sure brings back a lot of great memories."

"That's wonderful. I'd love to see it sometime, if you wouldn't mind showing it to me. I didn't really know my grandparents on either side. After my mom died, her parents didn't want much to do with me. I don't know if it was them or if my father pushed them away, like he did everyone else."

"I'm sorry to hear that. What about your dad's parents? Elise is your dad's sister, right?"

"Right. Their parents were distant people anyway. They were busy doing their own thing traveling all over the world even when Aunt Elise and my dad were growing up. Aunt Elise tried to fill in that gap for me after Mom died, but no one can do that entirely. Aunt Elise became more than my aunt and more like a mom. I couldn't have made it through losing my mother and having my father go off the deep end into work had it not been for her. She saved me. She raised me herself after my mother died giving birth to my little brother. My brother died shortly after that. I was only six."

"So...did Elise adopt you?"

"Oh no, she wouldn't have done that, even though I would've been fine with it. She always hoped my dad would come around one day and realize that he needed me as much as I needed him." Andi looked down and traced the wood grain on the table with her finger absently and let out a little sigh. "But it never happened. Kind of late, now, for him to figure that out."

Kelly fought the impulse to hold Andi in her arms to console her. She settled for saying, "That sounds like a sad childhood."

"Honestly, it sounds worse than it was. Aunt Elise made my life much, much nicer than it would've been if I'd been living with my dad. She's truly amazing. She always managed to balance a very hectic career with making sure I was taken care of and had quality time with her. She made time to come to nearly all my school events and to the teacher conferences. I couldn't have asked for a better surrogate parent."

"That sounds nice. You're lucky to have her. Did you see your father much?"

"Not really. I was only sad that he wasn't there when things like Father's Day rolled around and he didn't show up at all sometimes. You can see why Aunt Elise is my favorite person in the world. I'd tell you she's a wonderful woman, anyway, even if she was only a friend and wasn't my aunt. She's just so down to earth and loving."

"I'm surprised she never had any children of her own, since she obviously was a great mother figure in your life."

"Well, she's not the having kids herself kind. She did a great job with me, but didn't want any of her own."

"I'm glad you had someone in your life who made it easier. I can't imagine my childhood without my parents. I guess I was lucky in having them both around while I was growing up."

"You're very lucky." Andi let out a small sigh. "I guess that makes us both lucky in our own way. Do your parents live here?"

"No, they moved up to Ohio to be near my mom's sister after she had a stroke. Mom and Dad keep an eye on my aunt and help her out with things. Although they love me very much, my parents have never been very comfortable with who I am. So, having some distance between us works very well. By the way, I must admit I was surprised to see Elise out in the yard trimming her own trees. I'm sure she can afford to hire someone to do that." Kelly leaned back in the booth, her arm across the seat back's blue tapestry upholstery.

"Yes, she can. And she does, if it's something she can't do or doesn't have the time to do. But she likes doing things herself." Andi looked briefly out the window and then back at Kelly. "You know, she likes you. That means something in my book."

"I like her, too. I told her I don't take on every job that comes my way. If I don't hit it off with the customer, I just politely turn down the job. I usually tell them the job's more than I've got time to do right now. But, you know, the day I met Elise I knew I could work with and for her."

"She said she trusted you right away, too. The woman at the construction company that she uses gave her your name and told her you were an amazing woodworker. Aunt Elise told me she was prepared to say she'd wait till someone from the company could get to it, but she said she decided to meet with you and see what you were like. She figured she could always change her mind, then call the office back and say no, she'd wait for them to come do it. She told me last night she was glad she decided to meet you."

Kelly smiled. "I think it's going to work out well for both of us. She gets her bookcases the way she wants them and I get to work with some great people...you included."

Andi grinned back. "And I get a new friend. Works for me."

Their waiter arrived with pie and coffee for two, then with a cheery, "Enjoy," he left them to devour their desserts. Other than an occasional 'mmm...this is so good...' or a smile over a sip of coffee, neither of them said much. By the time the waiter brought the coffee pot over for refills, both were finishing their respective slices of pie and only crumbs remained on their plates.

"Now that was good," Andi said. "I wish I could bake like this."

"It's a good thing I can't. I'd bake pies all the time and be big as a house," Kelly said. "Not good."

"That's probably true for me, too. Pie's one of my biggest weaknesses, right up there with rocky road ice cream." Andi reached for the coffee creamer.

"Ah, then pie with ice cream would be the ultimate decadence for you." Kelly laughed. "I'm right there with you on that one." She took a sip of her coffee, leaned back in the booth, and gazed across the table. "I do need to introduce you to my friends Shawn and Carrie. Carrie's chocolate pie will put what you just had, good as it was, to shame."

"I'd love to meet them, especially Carrie. I admire people who can bake. I've always thought of baking as an art. Although I can take care of the basics, I'm not a very good cook, I'm afraid."

"Lots of people aren't much for cooking. It's either something you enjoy or you don't. I had a friend who never even turned on the stove in her house, and didn't plan to."

Andi smiled a little sheepish-looking smile. "It wasn't that I didn't like it. I just never did any cooking growing up, so it doesn't come naturally to me like it does to some people."

"Really? You never did any cooking at all?"

"Nope. We had a cook. That was one thing Aunt Elise always had help with while I was growing up. I guess she was afraid I wouldn't get enough nutritious food if someone else didn't take care of us. Aunt Elise can cook, but she was too busy to plan meals and make them when she got home from work. After I moved out on my own I found myself either ordering in or eating out a lot."

"Tell you what, I'll set something up and see if I can talk Carrie into inviting us over for one of her to-die-for pies." She leaned over to try to make eye contact with Andi. "As for not knowing how to cook, there are lots of people out there who are in the same boat as you for various reasons. That doesn't apply to me, of course. I'm a fairly good cook. I'll never starve as long as I can get to a grill." She chuckled. "Come on, you probably have lots of other talents."

Andi persisted in looking out the window and a little tear escaped her left eye. She quickly wiped it away, appearing to pretend it didn't happen. "You seem to have a good life, Kelly."

"I do. I've had my share of heartache, believe me. But overall, I think it's good. Someday I'd like to find someone to share it with on a permanent basis other than my dog, but I'm in no hurry. I'll never rush into something because I'm lonely. I hope you won't, either, speaking as a friend." Kelly reached over and patted Andi's hand once then withdrew her hand.

"I already made that mistake." Andi turned and looked at Kelly. "Never again. Next time, I'll make a commitment for the right reasons. The last one was a very big mistake, but I didn't realize it till I was in pretty deep."

"That's a bad way to learn a lesson, but I'm glad you learned from it. I've always figured that even a lousy experience is not a total loss if I learn something from it."

"True. Very true. Unfortunately, it's sad that we seem to need to get hurt to learn these things."

"I always figured I was too hard-headed to learn any other way." Kelly began to chuckle. "And believe me, I can be pretty hard-headed."

A smile inched across Andi's face, making its way to her eyes. "I bet you can be, Kelly. But I also bet you have a very tender heart. Tell me if I'm wrong about that..."

A blush crept up Kelly's neck to her cheeks. "I guess so. I like to think I care about people. If that means I have a tender heart, I guess I do." She looked at her coffee mug, and then back up at Andi. "I'm guessing you probably do, too. Someone has hurt you badly, but remember, not everyone's out to hurt you."

"I know that. But right now, I need to protect myself. I need to regroup and let myself heal. That's why I'm here, staying with Aunt Elise. She's my shelter from the storm. My rock. My haven. I don't know what I'd do without her." Andi stroked her finger around the rim of her coffee mug absently before draining the last of the caramel-colored liquid.

"She appears to be pretty solid herself. From what I've seen of her, she's very down-to-earth and she certainly cares about you. You're very lucky to have her in your life."

"I know I am." Andi reached for her keys lying on the table. "And I guess I'd better get going."

"Me too. I'll walk you to your car."

"Ah, my knight in shining armor to keep me safe, huh?" Andi smiled. "I like that. Thanks."

"I do seem to get called that. But it's really a safety thing...I want to be sure you get to your car all right." Kelly grinned widely. "Okay, and I want to get a look at that new car you're driving. Just curious."

Kelly could see Andi's rented deep metallic red Camry as soon as Andi clicked the unlock button on her key. Even in the parking lot light, it almost sparkled.

"Nice choice for a ride."

"I like it. I'm even thinking of buying one after I decide where I want to live."

"You mean you haven't decided where you want to live now? You said you have a business to go back to, so you must have a home and friends."

"Let's just say I'm not sure any more." Andi opened her car door, reached over and lightly kissed Kelly on the cheek. "I enjoyed this evening. Thanks."

"So did I. We can do this any time you like." Kelly laughed. "You know I like pie now. By the way, how do you feel about miniature golf?"

"I don't think I've played since I was a kid, but I remember it was fun. Why?"

"Well, it's something that might be entertaining to do some time. My friends suggested it. Anyway, it's an idea of somewhere to go if nothing else comes to mind and we're bored."

"We could do that. Oh, I almost forgot. Aunt Elise said she'd call you tomorrow about the latest options you gave her. I think she likes it even better. I better go. Night, Kelly."

"Thanks. Night, Andi." She watched Andi pull out of the parking lot, absently stroking her cheek where Andi's lips had touched her seconds before. She smiled faintly then grinned as she got into her Durango to drive home. She took a deep breath and started the engine. *This Andi could be dangerous. She might be hurt waiting to happen if I'm not careful.*

Chapter Nine

"ELISE, GOOD TO HEAR from you. What do you think about leaving off the cabinet doors on the end cabinets?" Kelly asked when Elise called her the next day. She put down the sanding block and wiped her hand on her shorts, then across her sweating face.

"I love your ideas, Kelly. I've been giving it some thought. I even sat at my desk and tried to envision the wall full of bookcases as you originally designed them with cabinets all the way across the bottom two shelves and as the alternate design with cabinet doors only on the middle three. I've decided I like your idea of having open shelves all the way down on the end bookcases. Every time I look over there, it seems like an even better idea. Let's change the plans to show the new design."

"I'm glad you still like the idea after thinking about it further. I'll redraw the plans so you can sign off on them, order the supplies, and get going as soon as I can. How about I bring over the final plans this afternoon? Is that okay?"

"That's fine. Wait. Even better, how about you come over for lunch. Andrea and I'd love your company and you can do two things at once."

"Very nice of you, I accept."

"Is twelve thirty good for you or would you prefer closer to one?"

"Twelve thirty is perfect. That'll give me enough time to redraw the plans and get cleaned up. Thanks for the invite. See you then."

Kelly ended the call and thirty minutes later, she had finished the changes to the drawings she made for the bookcases. She hurriedly got cleaned up and changed her clothes. She still had time to take the plans to get an extra copy made for Elise to keep.

Driving through the gate at Palm Harbour Isles was now beginning to feel familiar. She smiled and greeted the security guard as he gave her another dated placard for the Durango's window. As she drove toward Gulf Breeze Way, she realized how comfortable she was feeling around Elise. And Andi, too, for that matter. *Maybe I'm a little too comfortable. Elise and Andi are from a completely different background, socially if nothing else. Plus, Elise is my customer. I should be more business-like, but still friendly.* The instant Elise came to the door and greeted her with a hug, that thought went out the window.

"Kelly! I'm so glad you could come for lunch," Elise said releasing her. "We'll look at your drawings right after we eat, if that's all right." Without waiting for Kelly's response, Elise turned and over her shoulder said, "Andrea's just now finished putting out lunch. Let's not make her wait."

"Sounds good to me. Always a good idea to keep the cook happy."

They stepped into the kitchen as Andi finished laying out the food for everyone to make their own sandwiches—along with turkey, there was sourdough bread, two kinds of cheese, lettuce, tomato, mayo and mustard, and several kinds of chips, along with pickles and olives.

"Ah, buffet style. Fun," Kelly said. "No one can complain that she didn't get her sandwich exactly as she wants it."

Andi smiled. "That's the idea. Thanks for coming for lunch. It's nothing fancy, but it's filling."

"This all looks very tasty," Kelly said. "Thanks for inviting me."

They made their sandwiches, filling their plates with chips, pickles, and olives. They moved outside to eat on the lanai, where a pitcher of iced tea and a bucket of ice awaited them.

"It's so pleasant to eat out here," Elise said as soon as they were all seated. "When I designed this house, I wanted a large outdoor-feeling but indoor space where I could sit or entertain. What you see here is what I came up with and I've loved it from the first day."

"Elise, you continue to amaze me. You designed your own house?" Kelly asked, reaching for the iced tea pitcher.

"Well, I told the architect what I wanted and drew up the basic design myself. I knew how I wanted the house oriented on the lot and where I wanted each room to look out. I've added things here and there since then, but it's pretty much the same house as it was built."

Elise and Andi both held their glasses for Kelly to pour tea. "All I can say is, you did a wonderful job. It looks perfect." Kelly picked up her sandwich and took a bite. "Great turkey, too."

"Glad you like it." Andi grinned, looking directly into Kelly's eyes. "Sorry there's no pie to go with it, though."

Kelly felt her stomach do a little flutter. She mentally picked herself up off the floor and grinned back, trying to ignore what she felt. "I don't know about you, but I doubt I'll miss having some dessert after this very filling lunch. The next time you want pie, let me know and I'll be happy to go with you."

Kelly noticed Elise paying attention to their conversation, a little grin playing across her face as she watched them.

"Hey, I like pie, too," Elise said.

"Okay, Elise, next time we go out for dessert, you're invited along. How's that? I'm sure Andi doesn't mind at all."

Elise looked back and forth at the two of them. "Oh, so it's Andi, now, is it?" She chuckled. "Good. That means you at least like each other."

Andi looked pointedly at her aunt. "You know you're about the only one who calls me Andrea."

"I'm giving you a hard time, sweetie. I'm glad you two are becoming friends."

After finishing her sandwich and iced tea, Elise took a deep breath and pushed her chair away from the table. "All right, ladies, all done with lunch? Kelly and I need to talk business now."

"Sure. Do you want to see the final drawings out here? I laid them on the entry table."

Andi jumped up. "I'll go get them. You two sit right there."

Elise and Kelly looked at each other, Elise a bit wide-eyed with surprise. "Why, thank you, Andrea." Once Andi was out of earshot, Elise asked, "I don't know what's going on between the two of you, but she sure seems a lot happier since she got to know you. Just friends, right?"

"Of course. We've barely gotten to know each other. I do like her, though. She's fun to be around."

Andi returned to the lanai with the rolled-up drawings in her hand. "I did take a quick look at these. I like them." She grinned at Kelly. "That's strictly my opinion, and of course hers is the opinion that actually counts." She nodded toward Elise.

After Andi removed the luncheon items and dried the table, Elise and Kelly rolled out the plans for the bookcases. Elise ran her fingers over the drawings, seeming to feel them as Andi had done. Interesting. Kelly waited, giving Elise time to look at them in detail.

"Is there anything you'd like to ask me about them?"

"Tell you what, let's take them into my office for one more comparison. I want to be completely sure."

They rolled the plans back up and walked inside, through the living room and down the hall to Elise's office. Elise sat at her desk and held the drawing up, obviously imagining the view from her chair.

"I really like this. You've got a great eye and a wonderful design sense. I love the middle one being larger and deeper than the other four, giving the whole thing a design I hadn't thought of. The molding at the top and bottom of the pieces sets them off well and I also like the design on each shelf edge and the ends. They'll fit in here perfectly."

Kelly grinned. "I'm glad you like them."

"How soon do you think you'll start installing them?"

"I should be able to order the supplies this afternoon and start work on them in a few days. I plan to do the dirty work elsewhere and partially assemble them there. I should be ready to start putting them up in a couple of weeks. How does that sound?"

"Great. Now as to a down payment..." Elise sat down at her desk and pulled a checkbook from the drawer and began writing. "I'm really looking forward to seeing the finished product," she said as she tore off a check and handed it to Kelly. "Is this enough for a down payment?"

Kelly glanced at the check. It was for half the agreed-upon amount. "That's definitely enough, thank you." Kelly folded the check and put it in her pocket. "Before I do the final finish on them, I'll bring you a sample of how it will look so you can tell me if it's okay. I'd rather change what I'm doing before I start the finish than have to change it afterward. That's a lot of bookcases."

"I like that idea, too. Let me know once the sample is ready, or drop it off here if I'm not home. I'll be happy to get back to you right away."

Kelly studied the wall for a few seconds. "I just had another idea standing here looking at that wall. That's a very nice painting and it goes well with your office. Do you want to leave a space in that bookcase for it to stay there?"

"No, but thanks for noticing. I have another spot in mind for that piece of artwork. I'm looking forward to looking up and seeing all my books here, along with some of my other items that will look great on those shelves."

"Okay, we're good to go. I'd like you to sign off on them and I'll get to work. Oh, by the way, I do have an extra set of these drawings for you. I assumed you'd want them, since they'll be part of the house."

"Thank you, Kelly. I would like them." Elise signed and dated the bottom of the diagram. She tilted her head slightly and looked up at Kelly. "Do you have a minute to sit down for a chat?"

"Sure." Kelly rolled up the plans and settled into one of the armchairs across from Elise's desk. "What would you like to talk about?"

"It's Andrea." Elise leaned forward a bit and crossed her arms loosely with her elbows on her desk. "I know I sort of threw the two of you together a little, hoping she'd make a friend. I worried she was holed up here at the house or spending more time alone than she had to. Even the times she went out, she went alone."

Kelly smiled. "And we have made friends. I like Andi. She's fun to talk to."

Elise nodded. "Yes, she's sweet. I'm sure you understand she's vulnerable right now. I know you wouldn't take advantage of that vulnerability, but I had to say it."

"Elise, Andi and I are friends. I'd never take advantage of a friend for any reason at all."

"I didn't think you would, but again, I had to say it. Please be careful with her. I don't want her to jump into anything with anyone for a while. I can see you two like each other, but if anything, else came of your friendship right now, it'd simply be her on the rebound. I don't want either of you hurt, especially Andrea. She's been through enough. Does this make sense to you?"

"Makes all the sense in the world. Look, you have nothing to worry about. Andi and I are friends, that's all. She doesn't even live here, so we probably won't really become close friends before she's ready to go back home. I'm happy to keep her company, though, while she's here." Kelly looked closely at Elise. "Don't worry, nothing will happen. I've simply offered her someone to have pie and coffee or a drink with once in a while. I might invite her to come along to a friend's house for supper, how's that?"

"That sounds nice. I like you, Kelly. I don't think it would work out for the two of you to get very close, at least for the time being. I know she's a grownup now and she doesn't need me to take care of her, but she got burned badly the last time. She needs to heal first."

"No problem. I get it." Kelly stood up. "I should get going. I need to order the materials for your bookcases and I don't want to wait very late in the day to do it."

"I'm glad you understand. As you can see, I'm quite protective of Andrea." They stood up and Elise came around the desk. She placed her hand lightly on Kelly's arm. "I know I didn't really need to have this conversation, but I did it for my own peace of mind. Thanks for coming to lunch. And thanks just for being you. I know you understand."

"It's okay. I do understand, believe me. She's lucky to have someone care that much for her. Thanks for having me over for lunch.

I'm glad you like the plans and I'm sure we'll be seeing each other again soon. I'll let you know as soon as I'm ready to start installing the bookcases."

Kelly took a step toward the door, then turned back to Elise. "Oh, by the way, you'll want to take down that painting before we install your new bookcases and make sure the wall is in good shape. You don't want to have to patch the spot where the hanger was and paint it after they're in."

"Good idea. I'm glad you thought of that. I'll have someone take care of it tomorrow. Who knows, I might even decide to change the color of that wall."

Kelly turned again and strode toward the door. She stopped in the doorway and looked over her shoulder at Elise. "Don't worry about Andi. She's going to be fine."

"I know." Elise smiled.

Chapter Ten

"WHAT DID AUNT ELISE bend your ear about? I'm not paranoid or anything, but I had a feeling she was talking about me while she held you captive in her office."

Kelly laughed. "Captive, huh? Actually, it was mostly about the bookcases. But…she did mention that she was glad to see you coming out of your shell." Kelly moved her phone to her other ear.

"Really…interesting. That's so sweet. I know she worries about me."

"She obviously cares about you very much. I got the impression she's been concerned that you were holed up in the house too much, but I also got the feeling she understood why you might do that."

"What she didn't tell you is that she went through something like this years ago."

"She did?"

"Yeah. I know. Hard to believe. It was awful. She had her heart broken big time and went through a very crappy spell because of it."

"I'm sorry to hear that. It's hard to believe someone would want to hurt her. That could explain why she understands what's happening with you. Seriously, I can't imagine anyone wanting to hurt Elise. She's such a wonderful woman."

"Well, she…I guess I shouldn't say much more except that she probably worries more about me because of that. Whatever she says about me, it's good to hear it in that light. She's being very protective—maybe overprotective—but that's her."

"Thanks for the heads-up," Kelly said. "You know, everyone has a story. I think my friend Shawn said it perfectly. 'When you look at someone, you're only seeing the cover of their book. The real story is inside.'"

"I think that sounds very true. So, Kelly, what's your story?"

"Me? I don't really have a story. I'm the exception. I'm pretty sure I'm very boring."

"I doubt that. I can't imagine you being boring. Come on, tell me something about yourself. I know you like to make things out of wood, but you don't just hang around waiting for someone to need bookcases built, right?"

"No, I don't, but…"

"So, what do you do when you aren't building bookcases?" Andi pressed her.

"I buy houses, renovate them, and then sell them. I usually live in one of the ones I'm working on."

"That sounds interesting. How can you call yourself boring?"

"Well, it's not very glamorous, that's for sure. I work on them by myself, only contracting out the things I can't do or don't have the official credentials for. It takes time, but I get to make them look like I think they should and I don't have to deal with a crew…or a boss, either, for that matter."

"I knew you were talented. The drawing you did for Aunt Elise showed that you have quite an eye for detail. I'd even call you an artist of sorts. I think that drawing could almost be framed."

"That's kind of you. I'm not an artist, though. I just like making things."

"Come on, artists make things, too, you know. I'd love to see what you're working on some time."

"I'll try to arrange that for some time while you're still here. The staircase is kind of messed up right now since I had to take out the bannister and redo it. But if you're still around when I get the bannister back up, you can come over and see what I'm doing on this house."

"I think I'll probably still be around. I rather like it here."

"That's nice. I'm sure Elise likes having you here, too."

"She does. I'm lucky that she's used to having me under foot and I know I'm never intruding."

"From what she said to me, it sounds like she's planning to move here year-round soon."

"We'll see. She's talked about retiring before, but it didn't happen. Still, you never know. Well, I guess I'd better let you go, unless you have a yen for some more pie and coffee later."

"I doubt if that'll happen tonight, but it could happen tomorrow night. In fact, a pie craving can happen any time." Kelly chuckled. "Maybe I should keep some pie here on hand just in case."

"What? And have no reason to call up a friend to go out for coffee and dessert?" Andi was laughing.

"True. Very true. Besides, we promised Elise we'd invite her along on the next pie run. Don't forget about that. I bet she won't."

"You can take that bet. She doesn't forget anything. Besides, she's fun to be with."

"Yes, she is. She can come along any time as far as I'm concerned," Kelly said.

"Could we set it up for tomorrow night for dessert and coffee again? That way we could tell Aunt Elise ahead of time and she'll have something fun to look forward to, as well...I hope I'm not being presumptuous. I enjoyed the other night very much."

"No, no, you're not being pushy. I didn't have anything else planned for tomorrow night. See if Elise's good with that, then text me, okay? Let her know I'm fine with whatever time she'd like to meet there."

"Sounds good. Enjoy your evening." Andi's voice sounded husky.

"Are you okay, Andi?"

"Sure, I'm fine. I'll talk to Aunt Elise and get back to you later."

"Um...Andi, you can call me back if you want. It's okay. I assumed it'd be faster for you to text me."

"Thanks, I might do that." Andi's voice sounded almost normal again. "Catch you later."

Ten minutes later, a text message showed up on Kelly's phone.

8 pm tom at Perkins? Aunt Elise happy 2 b included. C u then.

She texted back, *Sounds great. See ya there.*

That was strange, Kelly thought. She texted back *Andi? Are you ok?*

Sure, I'm fine. See ya tom nite.

Why was Kelly getting the feeling something wasn't right? Andi obviously didn't want to talk to her about it, whatever it was. Couldn't be anything with Elise or Andi would've told her. Something was wrong.

Whatever it was, it happened right in the middle of their conversation. The little wheels in Kelly's brain churned even faster. Maybe Andi's ex texted her and said she wants to get back together. Maybe she said she's sorry and please come back home. That would explain Andi acting weird. Or it could be that she...never mind. She was sounding like a plot in one of Shawn's romance novels. She decided to let it go for now. If Andi wanted to tell her what was wrong, she would.

Chapter Eleven

WHILE TALKING WITH KELLY about meeting up the next evening, Andi's phone had showed another incoming call. It was a familiar number she hadn't seen for a while—Jo's. Andi decided to let it go to voicemail. She looked for a voicemail. Instead, she found a text from Jo. *You don't want to talk to me? That's fine. Filing for divorce. Hope that makes you happy.* Andi felt herself breathe in sharply.

"Anything wrong?" Elise asked her.

"Oh, no, nothing. Guess I'm just tired. Think I'll go lie down for a while and read." She gave Elise a hug. "You know I love you very much, right?"

Elise hugged her back and kissed her forehead. "Yes, I do. And I love you very much right back. You go read and relax."

Andi made a point to walk to her room at a normal pace and closed the door calmly. Safely alone, she flopped onto her bed and let the tears fall. Her body began to shake. She pulled her knees up into the fetal position as she let it out, her arms wrapped around a second pillow. All the frustration and anger she'd held in. All the hurt. Tears flooded down her cheeks as she sobbed into the pillow on her bed.

As the tears finally ran out, she wondered why she was so upset. She didn't think Jo was going to change and want to be the partner she should be. She wasn't going to suddenly realize she loved Andi and apologize for all the hurt she'd caused.

Andi sat up in the middle of the bed, the tissue box at hand. The answer came as an epiphany. It was the word divorce that caught her off guard. *I know I didn't want to go back to Jo, but until that text message I hadn't even considered the finality of a divorce. Now there's no going back. It's really over and I have to face this down and deal with it.*

Aunt Elise didn't even know about their marriage. Andi had never told her, and since the ceremony had been a simple courthouse thing, with wedding rings that didn't look like wedding rings, she'd been able to hide it from her. She knew Elise didn't approve of Jo and wouldn't have wanted to see her married to her.

Even though the wedding hadn't been what she would've liked, Andi had been in love. Everyone on the outside except Elise thought they were a great match. They ran in the same social circle, they were both well to do and loved art. Unfortunately, Jo was not romantic and although they usually slept in the same bed, they stopped having any kind of physical contact shortly after they married.

Andi knew she had to go back to New York and get a lawyer to represent her interests, since Jo was going to have one for hers. *Crap. I don't think I can explain this to Kelly without telling Aunt Elise as well, so I've got to come up with some story about why I must go back now. At least for Aunt Elise. I have no idea what to say to Kelly. It's time to make those plane reservations and get this thing moving.*

Chapter Twelve

KELLY PICKED UP HER phone. "Hey, Shawn. What's up?"

"Well, Carrie and I are wondering if you were planning to bring your new friend over to visit. Carrie says she'll make a chocolate pie...how about bringing her to supper?"

"As a matter of fact, I was telling Andi about Carrie's famous pie the other day and I know she'd love to have some. I doubt she'll say no when I ask her, unless she has something else planned."

"Great. You invite Andi and we can all enjoy an evening together. How's that?" Shawn sounded like she was stifling a laugh.

"Sounds like fun. But seriously, you must promise me you two won't start grilling her like you're my parents or something. You guys wouldn't do that, right?"

"Got it. Friends. No grilling." Shawn chuckled. "Okay, then, how about you ask her over for Thursday night? Carrie's dying to meet her."

"Okay, I will. You know I love Carrie's cooking. And one of her famous chocolate pies...well, I can't turn that down. If Andi can't come, I can still come without her, can't I?"

"I'm sure Carrie will be all right if you show up alone, but you make sure Andi gets invited and we'll make sure she doesn't feel grilled. Deal?"

"Deal. The usual, six p.m.?"

"Yep. By the way, did you finish that bannister you were working on?"

"Not yet. I've been spending most of my time on that project for Elise."

"So, it's Elise now, not Ms. Wainwright? Traveling in high society these days, are you?" Kelly could hear Shawn chuckling for sure, now.

"That's me. Seriously, of course not. She insisted I call her Elise. She's very nice, by the way."

"And the niece? Is she a lot like her aunt?"

"Well, in the beginning I wasn't sure about her. The day I first met her, she seemed rather cold and standoffish. After I got to know her a bit better, I realized that wasn't her at all. She was just trying to protect herself after being hurt. Now that I'm getting to know her, she seems very nice. I think she needs a friend right now, so I'm being friendly. Eventually she'll go back to New York, and I'll be someone who let her cry on her shoulder."

"Maybe not. You never know. So...you like her?"

"Yeah. I do. Not that I'm dating material for someone like her."

"What do you mean by someone like her?"

"You know. Rich. Lives in New York City."

"So?"

"So? Not even going there. She's not the piemaking-enjoy-evenings-at-home kind of woman, I'm guessing. She probably goes out all the time, has her picture in the society pages, that kind of thing. Not my kind of life. Definitely not living in New York. Never."

"What if she wanted to move here?"

"I doubt that would happen. This is a nice area of Florida and all, but compared to New York City, it's a backwater town."

"So, you've written her off already?"

"I pretty much have, at least for a potential relationship. Hey, I'll be her friend and all that, but I can't let those eyes of hers draw me in farther than friendship."

"Aha! You admit you're attracted to her."

Kelly could almost hear the huge grin from the other end. "Well, yeah. Wait till you see her. But I'm not letting myself get involved with her, no sir. As I said, she'll be out of here soon and I doubt I'll ever see her again."

"Maybe. Maybe not."

"I don't know about you, but I need to get back to work. Don't you have a character to kill off or a love scene to write or something?"

"Yeah, I guess I'd better get back to work, too. We'll see you Thursday evening at six, and if you can bring Andi with you, all the better. If not, we'll be happy to settle for your presence."

A few minutes later, Kelly called Andi. "Hey, there. I have an invitation for you."

"Hi yourself. I was going to call you in a minute. We need to cancel on the get together tonight. Unexpected company. But now you have my curiosity about the invitation."

"That's okay. We can do that another time. The invitation is from my friends Shawn and Carrie. They'd like me to bring you to dinner on Thursday night. Carrie's a fantastic cook and they'd like to meet my new friend...meaning you. Are you game for that?"

"Sure. Sounds like fun."

"It's not a date," Kelly quickly added.

"Nope, not a date. Friends having dinner with friends, right?"

"Yep, that's it. We're supposed to get there about six o'clock. As you know, everything down here's pretty much casual, so don't dress up or anything."

"Okay, I can manage that."

"By the way, Carrie's specialty is that luscious chocolate pie I was telling you about the other night at Perkins. Seriously, as I told you, it's amazing and she's making one for dessert Thursday, so we rank."

"I'm looking forward to meeting your friends, Kelly. Sounds like a fun evening."

"It will be. They're great people and I know you'll enjoy them. How about I pick you up about twenty to six?"

There was a little pause.

"I'm sensing hesitation. No problem. Would you rather meet at my house and we can go from here?"

"That sounds better. Not that I care if Aunt Elise knows we're going somewhere together, but...I'm thinking it seems less like a date that way. Especially to Aunt Elise."

"No worries. I'll text you my address and if you want to come over earlier it's okay with me. Call or text me that you're on your way."

"Sure. Actually, I'd love to see where you live."

"Honestly, there isn't a whole lot to see right now. I'm renovating the house I live in, so there's a bit of construction going on. I'd be happy to show some of it to you. And you can meet my little girl."

"You have a daughter?"

Kelly laughed. "She thinks she is. She's the four-legged variety. I've no idea what all she is, but according to the vet she's part Chihuahua, part Jack Russell, and who knows what else. She's all sweetheart. You don't have a problem with dogs, do you?"

"Oh, no. In fact, I love dogs. I'm looking forward to meeting your little one. What's her name?"

"Piper. That was her name when I got her and it seems to fit. As I said before, you can come over early if you like."

"Great. I'll see you tomorrow night."

Chapter Thirteen

THURSDAY AFTERNOON ABOUT FOUR thirty, Kelly's phone rang. "Is it okay if I come over early? I thought since I was going to get a house tour, it would be a good idea to have some extra time."

"Sure. I'm ready to go anyway. Come on over and I'll give you the grand tour of what's finished. We should even have some time for a glass of iced tea or something else if you like, before we go."

Fifteen minutes later, Andi pulled up in front of Kelly's house. Piper ran to the door to greet whoever was coming. After Kelly let her in, the first thing Andi did was bend down to say hi to Piper, who was turning in fast circles like a whirling dervish. She stopped once Andi put her hand out for Piper to smell. Having passed the smell test, Andi could pick her up and became the object of Piper kisses on her face.

"Piper, now that's enough!" Kelly reached for the little dog. "Not everyone likes that many kisses."

"I love dog kisses. She's adorable," Andi said as she handed Piper over.

Andi looked around the small living room and sighed. "Very cozy. Your house looks larger than most of the New York City apartments I'm used to. Bigger but still comfortable. I like it. I've always dreamed of owning a house like this. I will...one of these days."

"I'm glad you like it. This one's a work in progress." Kelly held Piper in her arms. "I'm sure you noticed the missing stair bannister. I had to rebuild it and I'll probably reinstall it tomorrow. Meantime, I don't travel the stairs much if I can avoid it."

"Since I've seen what you're capable of, I'm sure that bannister will be something great, not purely something to hold onto up and down the stairs."

"Yeah, I wanted to make it special, since it'll be used a lot...especially by the next owner."

"The next owner? Don't you plan to live here?"

"It's what I do. I buy houses, live in them while I fix them up, sell them, and move on to the next one."

"I'd hate to have to move out of this house. It already feels like home to me."

Kelly smiled. "That's the idea...to make them feel like someone would want to live in them. It's my specialty."

"Well, you do a great job. This house is lovely now and you said you're not finished with it. I could live in a place like this, easily."

"Too bad it's not in New York, right?" Kelly said.

"Yeah, I guess so." Andi let out a little sigh again. "Never know, though. I might want a place here like Aunt Elise has."

"How about some of that tea I promised you. Or I have other beverages if you'd prefer, but I give you my word I make pretty darn good iced tea."

"Then I'll have some tea and you tell me about your friends that I'm going to meet over dinner."

"Come on back to the kitchen and I'll do just that." Kelly put Piper down and led the way to the kitchen in the rear of the house, with windows facing the back yard. She motioned for Andi to sit at a small built-in dinette beneath one of the yard-facing windows. The late afternoon sun's rays dancing on the wood tabletop made the undulating sections of different colored woods seem to flow like creeks across the table.

While Kelly got the glasses from the cupboard and the pitcher from the fridge, Andi ran her hands over the tabletop. "This is gorgeous, Kelly. You did this, didn't you?"

"Yeah, I enjoyed making that. Taking different kinds of wood and combining them into a design is kind of my specialty." She sat down across from Andi. "I had a great time with this one." She ran her hand over it as well in an almost caressing gesture and smiled.

"You're very good at what you do. No wonder the construction company recommended you for my aunt's bookcases."

Kelly grinned. "Thanks. You're going to meet my closest friends this evening. Carrie's the office manager for that construction company your aunt uses and she's the one that recommended me to Elise. She also knows I don't take on many jobs like that." Kelly poured them both some iced tea as Piper jumped up on the bench next to her and laid down.

"I can imagine you don't have much time for other jobs, do you?" Andi took a sip of her tea, then held up the glass in a salute. "Nice."

"Thanks. You're right, I don't have a lot of time for extra jobs. Besides that, I'm quite particular about how something's made. If I hadn't had some design leeway on those bookcases, I wouldn't have agreed to the project. I don't throw something together, as you can see. Everything I make has to be something worth spending my time on and something worth having for a long time."

"I can see that. This house is unique. I'd bet you don't have any trouble selling them after you're finished, do you?"

"Not to brag, but no I really don't and what's more, I enjoy what I do. I'm sure you enjoy what you do, too, right?"

Andi looked down at her glass as if contemplating the ice cubes, then back up at Kelly. "I'd say I enjoy it most of the time. So back to Shawn and Carrie. Tell me about them."

"Shawn's a writer. She writes romance novels and other stuff. Carrie, as you already know, works at the construction company. They were married last year and I was Shawn's 'best woman' I guess you would say." She took a deep breath and looked away, gazing out the window. "They have a great relationship...something I'd like to have one of these days."

"That good, huh?" Andi sighed. "That sounds wonderful."

Kelly looked back at Andi. "That good. Honestly. Somehow, they mesh perfectly. They adore each other. Oh, and Carrie's a wonderful cook. I don't know what she's making for supper, but just you wait. Whatever it is, it'll be something wonderful. You can bet on that."

"Now I'm really looking forward to meeting them and getting a chance to sample her cooking."

"That's not the half of it. Wait till you taste some of that dessert I told you about. Seriously, it's to die for."

"I think you mentioned something like that before and I also happened to mention that I love chocolate pie, didn't I?" Andi was grinning again.

"I believe you did, as a matter of fact."

Chapter Fourteen

SHAWN WAS AT THE door, opening it as soon as Kelly and Andi were on the porch. "Come on in, you two. Carrie will be out in a second." Shawn greeted Kelly with a hug before turning to Andi. "And you must be Andi. Nice to meet you." She stuck out her hand to shake hands, which Andi took.

Carrie came into the living room wiping her hands on a dish towel, smiling. Carrie tossed the dish towel onto a side table before she hugged Kelly. "Thanks for coming. I know it hasn't been that long since we've seen you, but I still missed you."

"I've missed you guys, too. I've been busy lately."

"I know, it happens. You must eat and you know you're always welcome for supper. All you have to do is show up. There's always more than enough. Well, you're supposed to bring Piper with you, of course. Tonight, I'll send home some food for your poor, starving little girl." Carrie patted Kelly on the cheek and released her.

As Shawn put her arm around Carrie's waist, Carrie reached one of her now dried hands out to Andi, "Hi, I'm Carrie. I'm so glad you could come to dinner."

Andi grinned and shook Carrie's hand. "And I've heard a lot about you and your cooking from Kelly. She's been raving about your wonderful chocolate pie, as well."

"It's one of Shawn's and Kelly's favorites and we're having one for dessert. Hope you like it, too."

"Oh, I'm a huge fan of chocolate pie. I'm looking forward to it. So, Carrie, can I help you with anything? I'm not extremely useful in the kitchen, but I can follow orders well."

"Sure, come on back. We'll let Shawn and Kelly chat while we finish up with supper. Okay with you two?"

"Um...sure. Carrie, don't tell her anything embarrassing. We're new friends and I don't want to scare her away." Kelly looked stricken, but then laughed.

"Sure. I'll be nice." Carrie grinned at Kelly and reached for the dish towel on the side table "Come on, Andi, let's get dinner on the table so we can keep an eye on these two."

"You bet. Besides, I'm getting hungrier by the minute, with all those delicious aromas coming from the kitchen."

Once Carrie and Andi were out of earshot, Kelly plopped into one of the overstuffed chairs and Shawn onto the sofa. "Well, what do you think so far?"

"So far? Let's see. She's cute, she's charming, and she seems quite nice." Shawn grinned. "Hey, she even wanted to help out in the kitchen, it looks like. Not bad."

"Yeah, not bad for a rich girl."

"Rich girl? She doesn't seem like some snobby rich girl. I guess I shouldn't have said that. Not all rich people are snobby."

"No, she doesn't come off like that. Her aunt raised her, mostly."

"Is the aunt just here for the winter, then...a snowbird?"

"The aunt's a snowbird now, but getting ready to make Florida her year-round home. That's what the bookcases are for, to bring her considerable library here. They both live in New York City. Andi's connected to an art gallery there. The aunt's with a New York publishing house...an editor or the like, I believe. I get the impression they come from old money on the aunt's side of the family."

"Hmm...do you know which one? I mean, which publisher? I wonder if AJ knows her."

"I never thought to ask, to tell you the truth. It's very possible your publisher might know her or at least know of her. Her name's Elise Wainwright."

"I think I'll look her up after you guys leave this evening. I have a little niggling feeling that I've heard her name somewhere. Anyway, so back to Andi. You really like her now, or just friends?"

"I do like her a lot, but I don't see any future in this. She's from New York. The city. Big city girl. I don't see her moving here to stay."

"Are you sure you don't want to move there? She sure is cute."

"Oh, no...not me. I'm not the megacity kind of person, as you well know." Kelly put her hands up in a stay back kind of position. "I like it where I am, thank you very much."

"Let's just say you never know where life will lead you. I agree with you on the big city thing, though. I got tired of it, myself. I love it here and I'm glad I found someone who's happy here, too."

"Yeah, why can't I find a sweet local girl? Maybe I'm not in the right place at the right time. Perhaps it isn't my turn yet." Kelly shook her head. "I hope my turn comes soon—I'm not getting any younger." She laughed.

"No, you're not, but you're not ready for the retirement home, either. The right one's out there for you, I have a good feeling about it. Who knows, Andi could be the right one and you don't know it yet. She could be ready to give up big city life. She appears to be sweet, so far. You've spent time with her and you seem happy hanging out with her. Who knows...just let things take their course. Even if things don't work out for more between you, you do enjoy her company."

"True. Very true."

Carrie and Andi reappeared. "Anyone else ready to eat besides us?" Carrie asked.

"Oh, yeah. You don't have to ask me twice, that's for sure." Kelly jumped up and grabbed Shawn by the arm, practically flinging her to her feet and making her laugh.

"Me neither." Shawn walked over and gave Carrie a little kiss. "I'm sure it's wonderful, as usual, honey."

There on the table were dishes of roast beef, steamed broccoli with cheese sauce, mashed potatoes, and gravy. Kelly said, "Wow, Carrie, you went all out on this dinner. I feel special."

"Most of it was in the slow cooker all day, along with the potatoes. It wasn't as big a deal as you might think. You are special. You'll always be special." She reached over and patted Kelly's arm.

Kelly blushed.

"Isn't she cute? I love it every time she does that." Carrie giggled.

"She's very cute," Andi said, looking right at Kelly.

"Oh, now, stop it. I hate it when I blush," Kelly said, her hands rubbing her cheeks and staring at her plate as she sat down. "Makes me look kind of silly."

"I don't think so," Carrie said. "I think it makes you rather appealing and sweet. Don't you think so, Andi?"

Now it was Andi's turn to blush. "I do. But I think we should stop doing this to her, or she'll never get to eat anything."

"Yes, please." Kelly shook her head, trying to appear once more composed. "I'm starving and all you two want to do is make fun of me."

"Oh, come on, Kelly," Shawn said. "You know you love attention from lovely ladies. But you're right. Let's get on with dinner." She held her fork and knife up like she was ready to eat, making everyone laugh.

As they passed the dishes around and chatted, Kelly watched as Andi got into the conversations, laughing and joking like they were all old friends. That was great to see. Andi appeared to be enjoying herself and Shawn and Carrie seemed to be enjoying Andi. And she was enjoying Andi as well. She could feel it every time Andi looked over at her. Sometimes during conversations Andi would reach over and touch her arm, sending an unexpected chill the first time and something warmer after that.

***

Andi was totally immersed in the conversation over Carrie's chocolate pie when she realized this was the first time in a while she hadn't even thought about Jo. She glanced over at Kelly, who was laughing at another one of Shawn's stories about camping with her publisher and friend AJ. This one had something to do with a spider landing on Shawn's head. This was no fake, polite laughter here. This was the real, straight from the gut, tears running down the face belly laugh from all of them.

I love this. This is what I've always wanted and I'd love to continue to be a part of it. She glanced over at Kelly. *I know I'm having more than friendly feelings for her, but I must keep this in check as long as I'm still married to Jo. It wouldn't be right otherwise.* She was snapped out of her reverie by Kelly's voice.

"So, Andi, isn't this pie everything I said it is?"

Before Andi could answer, Carrie jumped in. "Come on, Kelly, not everyone loves it as much as you two do."

Andi put her fork down. "Carrie, this really is, as Kelly so aptly put it, to die for. I can't imagine how you get that crust to come out so flaky but I sure love the result. It's perfect. Now I know why Kelly's eyes glazed over as soon as she started talking about it the other day." Andi grinned at Kelly as Kelly started to blush once again.

"That's what Shawn does, too. I think this pie's what got Shawn's attention." Carrie leaned over to place a kiss on Shawn's cheek.

"Well, it didn't hurt, that's for sure. But I'd love you even if you didn't bake at all." Shawn returned the kiss sweetly, making Carrie smile. Shawn put the last bite of her pie in her mouth and sighed. "Yep, I do love this stuff. Good thing she doesn't make it every day. There's no way we could run or bike enough to work it off."

Andi watched the exchange between Carrie and Shawn and let out a tiny involuntary sigh. *This is what it's supposed to be like. It's what I want: a nice, uncomplicated, loving relationship.* She glanced over at

Kelly, she saw the same look on Kelly's face—that same bit of longing. *She wants the same thing. I know if we let it, we could have a wonderful relationship like theirs. But it probably can't happen. I must go back to New York and get a divorce and run a business. I have a life there. Or do I?*

After supper was over, the table cleared, and the dishes done with everyone's help, they adjourned to the living room. Andi had barely noticed the living room when they first arrived, other than it was cozy and inviting. This time her eyes were drawn straight to a lovely wooden rocking chair.

"What a gorgeous rocking chair you have. Is that a family heirloom?"

Shawn smiled. "It's fairly new, but it'll be a family heirloom from now on. Kelly made it for Carrie. We love it."

"Go ahead and sit in it, Andi." Carrie waved her over. "It isn't fragile."

Andi eased herself into it, caressing the wood in the chair arms. "This chair is amazing. The wood feels like satin." She leaned back into the chair. "What a wonderful present."

"There's a great story behind this chair," Kelly said.

"Of course. That makes it even better." Andi began to slowly rock, her head back against the headrest.

"The wood for this chair came from a tree that grew in Carrie's yard. Last fall a hurricane brought down the beautiful old tree that Carrie's grandfather had planted there."

As the rest of them sat down, Carrie resumed the story. "My grandparents bought the house two doors down from us right after they were first married and he planted that tree out in the front yard soon after they moved in. They lived in that house for decades and raised my mother there. After my grandfather died, my grandmother started calling that tree George, after him. She'd go talk to George whenever she felt sad or lonely, and it made her feel better." Shawn reached over and held Carrie's hand.

"I spent a lot of time with my grandmother and played in that tree as a child, the same as my mom. Grandmother died several years ago and left the house to me. I was living there at the time I met Shawn. Last year Hurricane Grace came through, Shawn and I went through the storm together there. It was during that storm that George came down."

"Oh, no." Andi stopped rocking.

Shawn chimed in, "Yeah, there he was, lying there with his root-feet sticking up and a big hole in the ground where he had lived all those years. It was heartbreaking to see. Carrie had the idea to call Kelly to see if she could make something out of part of the wood from that tree, so she'd have something to remember her grandparents by."

Kelly leaned forward. "I came over with my chainsaw as soon as the storm was over and I took some of the wood home with me. I spent a while trying to figure out what to do with it. It had to be something useful, something that wouldn't just sit in a corner. I wanted it to be something that when Carrie used it she'd feel close to her grandparents. So, I came up with the idea for the rocker."

"And it turned out wonderfully, as you can see," Carrie said.

"I tried to make it her size, so she'd feel comfortable in it. I made sure the back and arms curved in a way that it would almost give her a hug each time she sat in it and remembered her grandparents."

"And I do. Every single time. I love it. We both love it." Carrie looked over at Shawn, who was nodding. She noticed Andi was rocking slowly and listening with her eyes almost closed. "It's an amazing place to sit, isn't it, Andi?"

"It sure is." Andi opened her eyes and sat upright. "It's almost hypnotic, rocking in it, the rockers are so smooth. Kelly, it's such a...well, I've run out of words. It's definitely amazing and such a lovely thing to do for your friends."

"It was a labor of love, believe me. I enjoyed doing it." Kelly smiled at Carrie and Shawn.

"That's not the only thing she built for us." Carrie got up and went over to a shelf by the fireplace. She picked up a wooden box and handed it to Andi. "She made this for us as a wedding present."

Andi ran her hands over the exquisitely made box, with two different colors of wood pieced seamlessly together as if one. "What an interesting box. Those are your initials carved so intricately into the top, right?"

"Yes, they are. It's our treasure box." Shawn smiled at Carrie. When we go somewhere we pick up little things to remind us of where we've been."

"There was a bit left from Carrie's tree, so I went over to Shawn's yard and took a bit from one of the older trees there and combined them. It seemed fitting. The two trees had been growing there at the same time and now Carrie and Shawn would grow a life together."

"That's very romantic," Andi said. "Wow. Before now, I had no idea such romance existed outside of romance novels. I've read tons of them, but never had firsthand experience with it." She sighed and leaned back against the rocking chair again. "Such a wonderful thing."

"Well, we think so. You never know where you'll find 'the one,' do you?" Shawn winked at Carrie. "Could be right down the street." She laughed.

Andi examined the box further. "I had a thought. Kelly, have you ever considered making things like this for other people? I mean, custom made treasure boxes with their initials in them. I bet they'd sell very well."

Kelly shook her head. "Oh, no. That was a one off. I can't imagine doing it again. It was a fair amount of work for a little box. No one would want to pay enough for that. Besides, it was, again, a labor of love and I enjoyed making it. I don't like making things like that for money."

"I'm sorry, I didn't mean it like that. I guess I was thinking of other couples who'd love to own something like this. I mean, if I was getting married, I know I'd love a box like this." Andi ran her hands over the box absently.

"I hadn't really thought of that. To tell you the truth, I stay busy doing other things. The house keeps me very occupied and of course there are the few outside jobs I take on."

"Well, if you ever decide to make some more of these boxes, let me know. I'm sure I could help you market them. This isn't the time to get into that, anyway. That was my gallery voice. Whenever I see beautiful things like that, I hear my gallery voice coming on. I didn't mean to offend you in any way, believe me."

"Oh, I'm not offended. It's okay," Kelly said.

"Well, I can understand someone else wanting one of these," Carrie said. "What makes it so special for us is that Kelly made it and it came from the wood from our two trees. That can't be duplicated. For other people, it would simply be a box with their initials carved into the top. It might not be nearly as special."

"That's true." Andi laid the box gently on the table next to her. "Not everyone has as interesting a story as you two. I'm guessing the business about 'down the street' has something to do with how you met?"

Carrie chuckled. "It does, for sure."

"Carrie and I first met at the local grocery store, believe it or not. She literally fell into my arms at Publix." Shawn started laughing.

"Well, I fell, anyway, and you were courteous enough to catch me. I was mortified. It wasn't till later that we realized we lived down the street from each other."

"You actually fell for each other." Andi grinned. "How cute."

Carrie nodded her head. "I guess it was cute in hindsight, but it didn't seem like it at the time. Another coincidence was Shawn hiring the construction company I work for to add on a room and do some other work to her house. We got to know each other after that. But it was all coincidence. Her cousin had done some computer work for us and recommended us."

"Interesting. Guess you never know what's going to happen in your life, do you? I love the part about actually falling for her in the grocery store. That does sound like the beginning of a romance novel."

Shawn spoke up. "So, do you read a lot?"

Andi nodded. "I do. I especially love romances. My favorite author is S.K. Richardson. Have you guys read her stuff?" Shawn, Carrie, and Kelly started snickering before bursting into laughter, making Andi look around bewildered. She sat forward in her chair. "What? Did I say something funny?"

"No, you didn't." Kelly reached over and patted Andi's arm. "She's our favorite author, too." Kelly wiped the tears from her eyes.

"What, then? I don't get it." Andi still looked stricken. "Come on, tell me."

Carrie put her hand on Shawn's arm. "All right, honey, don't leave her hanging. Tell her."

Shawn laughed. "Andi, I'm S.K. Richardson."

"What? Really? Oh. My. God. I can't believe it." Andi leaned back in the chair. "Shawn, I've read every one of your books. In fact, I've read most of them multiple times. Wow. Just wow."

"Well, thank you. S.K. Richardson is my pen name."

"I'm so excited to meet you. I wish I had my copy of your last book with me for an autograph, but I left it in New York when I came down."

"Wait a minute." Shawn went to her office and returned with a pristine copy of *The Beach House* and a Sharpie marker. She sat back down on the sofa, opened the cover, and wrote something on the title page. She briefly blew on the writing, closed the book and handed it to Andi. "Here you go, with my compliments."

Andi stared at Shawn as she signed the book and handed it to her. She looked at it for a few seconds, gently opening the cover as if it was so precious it would break. There was the inscription: "For Andi. May you always be as happy as you look tonight and may you always have romance in your life. S.K. Richardson."

Andi felt a tear form in her left eye, then her right. She reached up to brush them both away. "Thank you very much. I really appreciate this and I'll always treasure it."

"You're welcome. It's always a pleasure to meet a fan." Shawn smiled at her.

"Aw, now, don't get all doe-eyed over meeting Shawn," Kelly said. "She's just someone who makes her living with words, like I do with wood. If you'd known her as long as I have, you wouldn't be so amazed at meeting her." She laughed. "I'm kidding, of course. She's very talented, isn't she?"

"Absolutely." Andi looked back at Shawn. "I do love your books. Sometimes if I've been having a bad day or just feeling lonely I've pulled one of your books off the shelf and read about someone else's romance and felt like there was a chance for me after all."

"Thanks for telling me," Shawn said. "I'm glad they were there for you."

Carrie put her hand on Shawn's thigh and patted it. "Believe me, I know how you feel. I'm also a huge fan of her books. Imagine how shocked I was when I realized who she was and that my favorite author was the woman living two doors down from me. I have to admit, though..." She took Shawn's hand and kissed it. "It was a very pleasant shock."

Shawn put her arm around Carrie. "You know, I've spent a lot of time protecting my privacy here in Florida. I wanted to be loved for me. I think we were already falling for each other before she realized who I was. It scared me anyway." Shawn's hand caressed Carrie's shoulder absently. "But we got it all straightened out. And we've got our own 'happy ever after' now, don't we, honey?"

"Yep. We do. I think the world would be a much nicer place if everyone had someone to love like this. We sure are happy."

"I can see that you are. I hope I find that, too." Andi grinned at Kelly. "Never know where the right one will turn up, do you?"

Chapter Fifteen

"SO, WHAT DID YOU think of Andi?" Shawn asked Carrie as they watched Kelly drive away with Andi into the darkening evening. "You spent a little one-on-one time with her in the kitchen."

"I think she's very nice. I got the impression that she's definitely a big city girl who's fascinated with our comparatively small-town life here. She jumped right in with setting the table, so she's definitely not some spoiled thing."

"I can hear a 'but' somewhere in there."

"But...well, I get the feeling she might be looking for the next thing for her gallery. You heard her talking about how those boxes would sell."

"I did. But I think she sounded like a businesswoman. She enjoys things then looks at them for their potential if they're something her gallery might handle." Shawn put her arm around Carrie's waist as they turned and walked back to the porch.

Carrie stopped on the porch. "Hmm...well, you could be right. I just hope Kelly isn't too stuck on her and gets her heart broken. She isn't staying, you know. She's heading back to New York soon, back to her society friends and all, you can bet on it." She opened the house door and they went inside.

"And? I got the impression she really likes Kelly, from some of the things she said and how she acted around her." Shawn pushed the door closed behind them.

"Oh, I'm not saying she doesn't like Kelly. I think she likes our Kelly a lot. But liking and more than that is a big step. I'm not sure she's one to take that bigger step with Kelly when there are such big gaps between them...financial, not that that matters in the long run, and distance. Kelly's not moving to New York City. Seriously. I could never see her living there."

"True. Andi could run back to New York and write off this period as a pleasant little vacation. She could enjoy hanging around with Kelly without truly caring for her."

Carrie thought for a second. "On the other hand, I think there could be something there."

"I thought you just said..." Shawn looked at her pointedly.

"I did. But, and it's a big but, I saw something between them this evening. There's something there, whether they recognize it yet or not.
"

"I'm pretty sure I saw that, too. Kelly's definitely taken with Andi, from what I heard listening to Kelly talk about her while you guys were in the kitchen."

"Well, I guess we'll see how this plays out." Carrie stopped and leaned against the front door. "As I said, I like Andi. She seems like a nice person, but I hope she doesn't hurt Kelly. I'd hate to think something like that could happen. Either way, Kelly's enjoying being around Andi and I think they're good for each other...at least right now."

"I think so, too. I guess sometimes you have to take a chance and enjoy the ride for as long as it lasts. It's great to see Kelly with someone again."

"Yeah, it's been a long time." Shawn put her arm around Carrie. "You know, I think she's looking for someone like you."

Carrie's cheeks reddened. "Really? Well, Andi isn't much like me, is she? Kelly does seem to have a thing for damsels in distress, though. She's drawn to helping people and maybe that's part of the allure. It's the knight in shining armor thing that she has—and is very good at, by the way. Besides, we don't look anything alike or..."

Shawn cut her off. "I think it's more like someone sweet and sexy and smart. Like you."

"You think she's sexy, do you?" Carrie grinned and pulled Shawn closer.

"Oh, honey, not nearly as sexy as you—" Shawn was cut off by Carrie's lips on hers.

Chapter Sixteen

AS THEY WERE LEAVING Carrie and Shawn's home, Andi reached over and planted a little kiss on Kelly's cheek.

"Well, thanks. But what was that for?" Kelly smiled.

"I had a great time. Your friends are wonderful, Carrie's a great cook, and we had an outstanding dinner. Lots of reasons. Most of all, thank you for letting me see what a great relationship looks like."

"Seriously? Don't any of your friends have a relationship like that?" Kelly glanced at Andi, then returned her attention to the road.

"No, they don't. At least none that make it that obvious."

"Wow. I'm sorry. I guess I'm so used to them being like that, I assume that's what it's like when two people truly love each other."

"I sure hope so. That hasn't happened to me yet, but I'd sure like it."

"Me, too. You know, Shawn went through a bad relationship or four before finding Carrie. I think Carrie scared her a little."

"Really? Why? She doesn't seem scary to me. In fact, exactly the opposite. Carrie's probably one of the most easy-to-be-around people I've ever met."

"She scared Shawn. She wasn't used to someone loving her for herself. She was used to having women put on a show for her and tell her what she wanted to hear. She got used a lot before she found Carrie. Actually, I don't know if they'd be together if Carrie hadn't been so patient."

"What do you mean?"

"I'll tell you in a bit. First, though, if you don't have anything else planned to do this evening, how would you like to drive down to the beach? There's going to be a full moon tonight and it's very pretty over the Gulf."

"Thanks, I'd love to. And no, I've nothing else planned that doesn't involve you."

"Elise isn't expecting you back at a certain time or anything?"

"I'm not on a curfew, if that's what you're asking." Andi laughed softly. "You'd think we were a couple of teenagers and Elise was my mom. I'm sure she won't worry at all unless I don't return home tonight. She knows I'm safe with you, though."

"Okay...Um...I wasn't planning to keep you out all night, so I guess you won't be in any trouble with Elise. Let's run back to my house and let Piper out for a couple of minutes to do her thing. It won't take long, then we'll be on our way to the beach."

"And we'd better not forget to give her this doggie bag Carrie sent her." Andi held up the plastic container holding some roast beef and gravy intended for Piper.

"Oh, no. We can't forget that." Kelly laughed.

It didn't take long for Piper to take care of her business and have her ears scratched by both of them. With her treat from Aunt Carrie to chow down on, Piper wasn't unhappy to let them leave again.

A short time later, Kelly turned onto North Cleveland Avenue toward the bridge across the Caloosahatchee River. Andi patted Kelly's thigh briefly, "You know, I'm not worried about you keeping me out all night." She grinned.

Kelly swallowed hard, trying not to react to the touch of Andi's hand on her thigh, brief as it was. "Well, then...I guess we're good." Kelly couldn't look over at Andi. "We were talking about Shawn and Carrie, right?"

"Right. You were telling me about how they might not have gotten together if Carrie hadn't been so patient."

"That's right. So anyway, Shawn kept getting gun-shy around Carrie. They went out. They kissed. Shawn would run off every time things got any more heated than that. She was so scared of making another mistake that she almost let Carrie get away."

"What was she so worried about?"

"Mainly she was worried that if something went wrong, she'd have this ex lover living two doors down, making it very uncomfortable."

"Wow, she was thinking ahead, but that sounds a bit paranoid."

"Oh, you don't know what she went through with past relationships." Kelly shook her head. "It's not all that paranoid if you've been through what she has. Still, Carrie didn't know who Shawn was when they met, just that she was some kind of writer. And she only knew that at first because her company was building on a writer's retreat type office for Shawn's house."

"Carrie mentioned that this evening. She said she was shocked finding out who Shawn was."

"Yeah, Shawn said the turning point was Carrie talking to her about her books, and finally figuring out who she was. Until then, it had been a low key, normal fun thing but after that, it became Shawn's scary thing. She's been pursued by a few fans who were sure they were in love with her because of her books. It wasn't pretty."

"Well, I guess you don't get chased down by crazed women very often for your woodworking skills?" Andi giggled.

"Uh...no. Not even close." Kelly grinned as she glanced briefly at Andi. She moved to the inside lane right before they reached the Caloosahatchee River Bridge.

"By the way, Carrie did tell me something about you."

"Hmm...do I want to know what it was? I mean, you already know I love her cooking."

"I think you'll like to hear this, since it was a sweet compliment. She said you were her Lancelot. Knight in shining armor. Rescuer of damsels in distress."

Kelly could tell without even looking that Andi was grinning again as she recited and laughed. "She did, did she? I suppose that's somewhat true in her case. I did help a little getting them together finally, but I don't think I actually rescued her from anything."

"She thinks you did and I think it's sweet. Do you make a habit of coming to the aid of women in distress?"

Kelly heard Andi giggle and felt her own face redden, grateful for the darkness. "Uh...I don't know. Maybe. I hate to see someone upset if there's something I can do to help. If that makes me a knight in shining armor, I guess that part's true."

"You definitely came to my aid." Andi reached over and patted Kelly's thigh again lightly, starting a tingling rushing up Kelly's leg. Kelly blinked and tried to ignore those distracting sensations. "I think you can add me to the list of damsels in distress that you've saved."

"You simply looked like you needed a friend. I knew from what your aunt said that you didn't live here, so I thought you could use someone to talk to. That's all. I guess I can't resist beautiful women needing help." She laughed a bit nervously.

"You think I'm beautiful?" Andi asked softly.

Kelly looked over at Andi for a second, then back at the road. "I think you are. Don't you see that when you look in the mirror?"

"At one time, I supposed I was pretty." Andi let out a little sigh. "Now my mirror only shows me someone who's no longer in her twenties, tired of running around being something she isn't."

"I'm sorry to hear that. Maybe if you stopped trying to be what you aren't, you'd see that lovely woman everyone else sees."

Andi sighed. "Thank you, Kelly. You do seem to know exactly what to say to make me feel better."

"That isn't what I meant. I didn't say what I did to make you feel better. I meant every word of it. You are a beautiful woman. Your smile lights up a room and when you let go, your laughter is wonderful to hear. I love seeing you happy."

They turned left onto San Carlos Boulevard, which led directly to the beach. Brightly lit signs shaped like fish and anchors announced seafood restaurants along the road. Beach shops and marinas shared the rest of the ride to the bridge leading to the island beach.

Kelly broke the silence. "My mom told us there used to be a wooden bridge here. I can't even imagine that."

"It's great having history in a place, isn't it? Your parents and grandparents being here before you and all. That's very grounding."

"I guess it is, come to think of it. But your family's from New York City, right? Don't you have some of that there?"

"I guess you're right, but I hadn't thought of it that way. We've gone to some of the same restaurants Aunt Elise says her parents took her and my dad. She took me to the Museum of Modern Art and the big public library, like her mom took her. That kind of thing. I hadn't considered it in that way."

Kelly pulled into a parking lot overlooking Fort Myers Beach. The fat moon appeared to be only inches above the horizon, enough to make a lovely reflection on the water. She put the car window down a bit more to let in some of the gulf breeze, but not enough to chill them.

She looked at Andi. "So, what do you think of that? Isn't it beautiful?"

Andi leaned back in her seat and sighed. "Gorgeous. Worth the drive, to be sure. And quite romantic."

Kelly released a sigh. "Yes, it is. I love this spot and thought you might enjoy it."

"There's a bench over there. Want to sit outside and look at the water?"

"Okay, if you don't think you'll be too chilly. There's a bit of a breeze coming off the gulf."

"Oh, I'm sure I'll be warm enough."

They got out of the Durango and walked the thirty-odd feet across the sugary white sand. They both let out another sigh and smiled as they settled on the bench. At first, they sat not quite touching. Andi moved slightly closer until Kelly could feel their thighs touching. Kelly put her arm across the back of the bench behind Andi, all the while not actually looking at her. The swooshing and lapping sounds of the waves were accompanied by palm fronds rustling above them from the gulf breeze, which also brought the beach smells of seaweed and saltwater.

Kelly glanced over at Andi and the sight took her breath away. The moonlight on her face made her look like an angel. Her skin almost glowed. Her hair shone in the moonlight, small strands floating in puffs of air. *Oh, no, I'm not going to fall for that.* She looked quickly away, but couldn't help looking back again. Suddenly neither the moon nor the waves had as much attraction for her. When Andi looked back at her, she couldn't help gazing into those eyes.

Kelly's arm went around Andi, almost of its own accord, drawing her closer. Andi closed her eyes, inviting a kiss. She felt her lips meeting Andi's, soft and sweet. Just a brief kiss—a simple, gentle touching of lips that only lasted a few seconds—then Andi smiled and snuggled into Kelly's shoulder as Kelly's arm tightened around her.

Andi's head fit perfectly into that spot where Kelly's shoulder met her chest. As Andi snuggled in against Kelly's side, Kelly could feel her heart racing, each beat seemingly so loud anyone on the beach could hear it. She hoped Andi couldn't hear it though, giving away what she already knew—that she was feeling things for Andi she hadn't planned on. They sat there for a while longer in silence, listening to the waves rhythmically lap at the shore as the tide came in.

"We probably should head back," Kelly whispered.

Andi looked up at Kelly. "Yes, we probably should."

"I mean, you left your car at my place, so it'll take a while to get there. Afterward, you have the drive back to Elise's house..."

"Oh, yeah. That's right. I did leave my car there. I almost forgot." Andi stood up. "Well, I guess we'd better go."

They walked back to the car in silence, Kelly opening the door for Andi. As soon as they were back in the car, but before she started the engine, Kelly turned to her. "I probably shouldn't have kissed you. I'm sorry."

Andi looked down at her hands. "Don't be sorry. I liked it." She looked back up at Kelly. "It was nice. It was only a spur of the moment, moonlight kiss thing. No worries."

"Right. Exactly." Kelly took a deep breath. *Sure, it was. Now what?* She started the engine and they drove back without saying much.

After they returned to Kelly's house, Andi went straight to her car and after unlocking it, tossed her bag into the passenger seat. She turned around and put her arms around Kelly's waist.

"You really are a knight in shining armor. I feel like you've rescued me from myself."

"How's that?" Kelly could feel warmth creeping into her cheeks and elsewhere from the feel of Andi against her. Her arms went around Andi of their own accord and held her close.

"I was letting myself believe that I was unlovable." Andi's voice was husky, her cheek against Kelly's shoulder. "I assumed no one would want me around much without Jo. But you've let me see that I can have someone in my life that likes me for myself. Thank you for that."

"You're much more than that, Andi. You're a beautiful, intelligent woman who's fun to be with."

"Thank you for that, too. And for being my friend." Andi looked up and planted a little kiss on Kelly's cheek. "Thanks for the moonlit kiss, as well. I liked it. Maybe more than you did."

Before Kelly could reply, Andi released her. She got in her car quickly and started the engine. "Night, Kelly. I had a great time." She waved and backed out of the driveway. In another few seconds, she was a pair of taillights in the dark.

Kelly stood there watching those two red lights recede down the street as she softly stroked the place on her cheek where Andi had kissed her.

.

Chapter Seventeen

THE NEXT MORNING, ANDI'S bags were by the door as she and Elise sat in the kitchen nook. Andi picked at the cinnamon roll in front of her and sipped on her coffee. Elise sat with her elbows on the table, holding her mug with both hands as she sipped on it. She looked at Andi over her coffee mug.

"Are you sure you need to leave now? I thought you and Kelly…"

"Kelly and I are friends, Aunt Elise. That's it." Andi's voice was so soft, Elise barely heard her.

"Are you sure? I mean, I've seen the looks passing between the two of you. It might not be very easy to work out with her here and you there in New York, I guess. But I thought it looked like there was a connection between you."

Andi reached across the table and stroked her aunt's hand gently. "Even if there is something between us, it would never work out, as you say. Besides, I have a business to attend to."

"I'm sure you do. Not to be nosey, but you did tell Kelly you were leaving, didn't you?"

Andi picked off another bite of cinnamon roll, but only looked at the sticky icing on her fingers. "No, I didn't." She looked over at Elise and took a deep breath. She finally popped the piece of roll in her mouth and ate it. "We didn't have anything else planned to do together."

"So, did you enjoy your dinner last night? You said you were going to have supper with her friends."

"I had a wonderful time. Her friends were very nice." Andi licked the icing off her fingers. "Guess what, one of them writes as S.K. Richardson, my favorite author."

"What a coincidence. I know who she is, but I don't know her. That made the evening quite special for you, I'm sure."

"It was very special and I couldn't believe it at first. When I mentioned that I had a copy of her latest book at home, she even gave me an autographed copy. I'd already read it, so I'll pass on my copy back in New York but I'll treasure this one. I'll leave it here for now, with some of my things, since I'll be back shortly."

"Oh good. Do you think you'll be back in time for the big reveal? Kelly should be finished with the bookcases soon."

"I won't be gone long. Maybe two or three weeks."

Elise thought for a few seconds. "You can't go back to the loft, so where do you plan to stay? If you'd like or need to, you know you can stay at my place."

"I've already checked with my friend Sarah. She says I can stay in her spare room for now. It'll be fun, like when we were in college together. Plus, it'll be closer to the gallery."

I'm not really lying to Aunt Elise but I'm not telling her the whole truth, either. Thank goodness Sarah didn't ask a whole lot of questions and was happy to have me stay for a bit. I can't tell Aunt Elise that the big reason for going back is an appointment with my attorney. I want things settled once and for all with Jo. I know now that I want to be free.

***

On the plane a few hours later, Andi leaned her head back on the seat and closed her eyes, remembering that kiss in the moonlight with Kelly. She could almost feel the touch of Kelly's lips softly on hers. She sighed as a smile slowly stole across her whole face. She was sure Kelly felt more from that kiss than she was letting on. It felt perfect. It felt right. Andi was toast and she knew it.

But it would never work. Kelly won't leave Florida, and I don't blame her. I don't know if I could leave New York City for good, either. What can I do? I can't work one of SoHo's up and coming galleries from Florida. Or could I?

Or maybe I could start over in Florida. I have my name in the art community. Yes, it's possible. It could be done...a gallery there in Fort Myers or perhaps Naples? Naples isn't that far away. Anyway, it's a thought.

Could I be kidding myself that Kelly's genuinely interested in me? I can't press finding out until I am actually able to do something about it if she is. I do know one thing. I'd love to live in that house Kelly is renovating, even if it's as a vacation place. It feels like home. For the first time in my adult life, someplace other than Aunt Elise's feels like home. She dozed off on the plane, a trace of a smile still on her lips.

Chapter Eighteen

TWO DAYS AFTER ANDI left, Kelly called Elise to ask her a minor question about something on the bookcase wall. She hadn't heard from Andi and didn't want to push anything, but she decided to ask about her anyway.

"How's Andi today? I haven't heard from her since the other night."

"Andi went back to New York early yesterday morning. Didn't she tell you?"

"Well, no, she didn't mention leaving at all. Was there some kind of emergency?"

"Not that I know of. She said there were some things she needed to take care of at the gallery, but that's it. She's staying with a friend there. I'm sure you can reach her by phone if you'd like to talk to her."

"No, there's nothing to talk about I guess. Did she say anything about the other night?"

"She said you two had dinner with a couple of your friends. She did mention that one of them turned out to be her favorite author. Other than that, though, she didn't say a whole lot. She sounded like she enjoyed the evening, though."

"My friends said they really liked her and she seemed like she had a good time, but I haven't heard from her and I wondered if she was all right. It's no big deal but I thought since I was talking to you anyway that I'd check to see how she was." Kelly felt herself rambling.

"Why don't you just call her? You two have been chatting like crazy for a while now. It's no big deal. Call her."

"I will. Kind of busy right now, but I'll call her in a bit. Thanks for the info, Elise. I'll let you know as soon as the bookcases are finished."

"Call her. Soon." This sounded almost more like a command from someone's mom.

"Yes, ma'am. I will." Kelly smiled. *Yep, that sounded like a mom voice for sure.* She punched in Andi's number but her phone went straight to voicemail.

"Hi, this is Andrea Wainwright. Please leave a message and I'll get back to you right away."

"Hi Andi, this is Kelly. Well, you can tell it's me from the number on your voicemail, but anyway...I hadn't heard from you in a couple of days and wondered how you're doing. Elise says you're back in New York for a while. I guess you didn't have a chance to say goodbye or whatever. Hope everything's all right. Call me when you get a chance?"

After several hours went by without a return call, Kelly started thinking. *Maybe she's busy, but she could at least text me.*

As another day went by, her brain went into overdrive. *Maybe Andi really has been playing me along because she was lonely. Maybe that kiss the other night didn't mean anything other than she felt like being kissed. Or, well, maybe I'm reading more into that kiss than it was meant to be and I need to back off. That's it. Just back off. The project is nearly done and I could get it finished and installed and never have a reason to see Andi again. Maybe that's what I need to do, if I can.*

***

Kelly worked hard to get the bookcases finished. Three weeks later and the last day she was working on them at Elise's house, she looked up to find Andi standing there.

"Hi, Kelly. Nice job." Andi stood there for a minute longer looking everywhere but at Kelly.

"Thanks. It'll be finished in a few minutes." Kelly only glanced up again at Andi, but she was already gone. *Well, that settles that. Andi is back to business-like mode.* Kelly felt a little tug in her stomach but she pushed it back down and went back to work. A few seconds later, Kelly looked over at Elise, who'd been standing there watching Kelly do the final bits to the installation.

"I didn't know Andi was here," Kelly said.

"She came in very early this morning and I thought she was still sleeping when you got here. I assumed you'd be done before she got up, so I didn't say anything. I'm sorry. I guess I did a lot of assuming."

Kelly stood up, stepped back to look at the finished wall of bookcases and smiled. "That's all right, Elise. So, how do you like them?"

"They're beautiful. They're exactly as I envisioned them." She folded her arms, tilted her head, and looked at them off-kilter. "They almost look like a work of art. I love them."

"I'm happy if you're happy. I tried to make them fit in with the rest of your office furniture. I'm rather proud of how they turned out, too."

Elise walked around her desk and opened the desk drawer. She took out a check and handed it to Kelly. "How's that? I hope it's enough to tell you how much I love them."

Kelly looked at the check and she thought she'd need a shovel to scrape her jaw from the floor. The check was made out for an extra five hundred dollars more than they had settled on. "Wow, Elise. This is much more than we agreed to. I can't take this." She reached out to hand the check back, but Elise held her hand up in a stop motion.

"Yes, you can. Your work is worth every penny I've paid you, believe me. Now, put that check in your pocket and let's call it even." Elise grinned at her. "Besides, I'd like to be in your good graces in case I want something else done."

"Well—"

"Look, I know you made an exception for me to take on this job. Besides, I'm hoping you might make another one for me occasionally. I promise I wouldn't ask you to do anything boring, like a shelf over my washing machine." Elise placed her hand over her heart. "I also promise not to give out your name and number to any of my neighbors unless you say it's okay. Would it be all right if I called you directly to see if you're available the next time I need some woodworking done? Now that we're friends, it seems rather silly to go through the contractor again."

"I guess that would be okay." Kelly figured that she could always say no later and it wouldn't be nice to say no now to Elise. Besides, she liked the woman.

Elise reached out her arms for a hug, and with her arms around Kelly, thanked her again for the beautiful job she had done.

"Oh, one more thing." Elise released Kelly with a smile. "Do you think you might come for lunch with me occasionally? Just you and me as friends. I like you and enjoy your company. You're my kind of woman...interesting and fun to be around. I'd like to stay friends with you, not only do business."

"Sure, I'd love to. I like you, too." Kelly hoped Andi wouldn't be part of the deal if she came to lunch.

She was happy to get out the door without seeing Andi again. As she drove away, she told herself she didn't care to see Andi ever again. *Okay, at least not any time soon. I know I got a little too close to her and shouldn't have kissed her. At least nothing else happened.*

Chapter Nineteen

A WHITE CHRISTMAS IN New York City is magical. The shmoosh of the snow underfoot, the sounds of traffic and the bell ringers in front of the stores, and the aromas from the food carts all contribute to the enchantment that the City holds during the holidays. Andi loved looking at the beautifully decorated store windows as she walked or rode along the streets. The song 'Silver Bells' played on an endless loop in her head at this time of year. In all the Christmases since she first heard it as a child, she knew it must've been written with New York City in mind.

On her way to Elise's, she knew it was time to confess to her aunt what was going on. She didn't want to ruin dinner and vowed to wait until after they finished their Christmas meal. She didn't want to tell her before then and upset her or mess up their dinner. She rode up in the elevator, shopping bags in both hands, trying to plan what she'd say. No matter which way she figured her mind kept coming up with a blank. She sighed, hoping that when the time came, she'd figure something out.

There were only two homes on Elise's floor. Out the elevator doors and to the left was Mrs. Gandy. She'd been there for ages and stayed on after her husband died. She could afford to, since he left her comfortably taken care of. Andi placed a small gift bag on her doorstep and grinned. She'd been doing this since she was a little girl and Mrs. Gandy always got a kick out of it.

To the right was the door to Elise's. Andi pushed the familiar doorbell with her elbow. The second Elise opened the door, the aromas of turkey and apple pie as well as the yeasty aroma of fresh baked rolls enveloped Andi and almost made her swoon. She took a deep breath and reached out to embrace her aunt with bags in hand. "Merry Christmas, Aunt Elise."

"Oh, sweetie, I'm so glad you're here. This is what I always come back for. Don't you just love it?"

"That's obviously a trick question. You know I love it." Andi held her aunt close. "Christmas has always been my favorite holiday, especially Christmas with you."

Elise took the bags from Andi's hands and placed them on the marble-topped entry table. She wrapped her arm around Andi's waist, holding her close as she led her to the living room. There, as Andi knew it would be, was a gorgeously decorated Christmas tree that reached well over halfway to the ceiling of the two-story living room, holding court in front of huge windows that overlooked Central Park. Presents wrapped in silver and gold nestled beneath it, waiting to be opened.

Andi took a deep breath and put her arms around her aunt again, nestling into her warmth. "I love you so much, Aunt Elise. You're the one happy constant in my life. Merry Christmas."

"Merry Christmas, sweetie. I love you, too." Elise took Andi's hands in hers, feeling their chill. "Oh, you poor thing. Let's get you out of that coat and into a nice warm drink."

"That's what you always said every time I came home in the winter. I'm not that little girl any more, you know." She smiled. "You're one hundred percent correct. I could use something warm to drink."

"I thought so. Sophie made us some of her famous hot chocolate. We can always perk it up with something if you'd like."

"Sophie's hot chocolate's perfect the way it is. I wouldn't presume to put anything else in it. Besides, she'd kill us."

"Come to think of it, you're probably right. We shouldn't mess with perfection. Let's go find some of that magic liquid and wrap your hands around a warm mug to chase the chill away."

"Let me put those presents I brought under the tree first and I'll be right there." Andi went back to the entry and retrieved the bags. She carefully placed each beautifully wrapped package under the tree among the silver and gold wrapped items already there. She smiled. Aunt Elise traditionally wrapped everything in silver or gold. Andi always wrapped hers in red or green. No tags were needed unless they were for someone other than the two of them.

***

Several hours later, dinner completed and presents opened, they relaxed in front of the fireplace, each with a glass of wine. The only sound was the crackling of the logs as they burned.

"To many more happy Christmases," Elise said as she saluted Andi with her glass.

"Yes, to many more." Andi held her glass up in a return salute before taking a sip of the deep red merlot, and stared into the fire.

"Aunt Elise, there's something I need to talk to you about."

Elise's brows furrowed and her head tilted as she gave Andi her full attention. "You look serious. What's up?"

Andi took a deep breath and decided to blurt it out and get it over with. "I'm in the middle of getting a divorce from Jo."

"You're...what?" Elise set her wine on the smoked glass sofa table with a little clink. "When did you get married?"

Andi took another deep breath. "A couple of years ago. I guess I thought things would be better between us. She said she loved me and wanted to marry me." She blinked back a couple of tears.

"Oh sweetie, I'm so sorry. That's a bit of a shock, for sure." Elise shook her head. When she spoke again, it was almost a whisper. "I had no idea. Why didn't you tell me?"

"I knew you didn't like her. You only tolerated her for my sake."

"True, she wasn't one of my favorite people in the world, still...I wish you'd told me."

"Look, we didn't make a big deal of the wedding and only a few of our friends knew. It was sort of an impulse thing while we were on vacation. Jo had a small showing at a gallery in New Hope, Pennsylvania, and we got married there."

"I'm so sorry you're going through this." Elise reached for Andi's hand. "I know you loved her a lot more than she cared about you. That was clear from the beginning to me. But saying I told you so would be silly at this point, so I won't say it."

"I appreciate that, believe me." Andi managed a wan smile.

"Going through a relationship breakup was bad enough. Now you're going through a legal divorce as well."

"Yes, and believe me, it's not fun. Bet you never thought lesbians would be going through the same stuff everyone else does with a divorce. She hasn't talked to me at all herself since texting me that she wanted a divorce. That happened while I was visiting you."

"That explains why you had to take off like you did. You're right, I thought she took advantage of you and didn't treat you well. That's why I didn't care much for her and I can't say I was unhappy about your breakup. But I could tell things weren't the same between you the last time both of you were here. It never occurred to me that you two had married. Is there anything I can do to help?"

"I doubt it, although I appreciate the thought. My attorney says these things take time to run their course. I only have to wait for it all to happen now." Andi leaned back against the sofa with a sigh.

"I don't want you to think I'm butting in here, but I do know people who might be able to hurry this along or make it easier. Are you two in agreement about who gets what?"

"We're not fighting about anything, if that's what you mean. I think she's anxious to get this over with, too. At least, so far, she doesn't want half of my gallery. I hope not. I did that all on my own and started it before we were married. She probably wouldn't have much of a case." Andi sighed. "You never know about these things. If she knew I was interested in someone else, she could decide to drag this out by petitioning for half the gallery. It's the only thing she could use to delay the divorce. I'm glad now that we always had separate bank accounts. I feel silly now that we didn't have any kind of prenuptial agreement."

"Sounds like it isn't overly problematic right now. Tell you what, I'll make a couple of phone calls tomorrow and see if things can be hurried along so we can get you out of this and on with your own life. Putting this behind you as soon as possible is the best thing, don't you think?"

"That's true. I want to move on with my life and I can't till I feel I'm free from Jo."

"Just out of curiosity, does any of this moving on part possibly involve feeling something for Kelly?"

"Kelly?" Andi tried to give her aunt the 'I have no idea what you're talking about' look she'd used while she was a little girl.

Elise grinned at Andi. "Don't look at me like that, young lady. You know I always could read you like a book. Now, I could be totally wrong about this, since it's happened once or twice before." Elise winked at her niece. "I'm guessing you have feelings for Kelly. Am I right?"

Andi looked a bit sheepish. "I like Kelly a lot. You and I have talked about this before...I can't see how it would ever work."

"So that's why you took off in a hurry when you did? You could've at least texted her or called her to say goodbye, as a friend if nothing else. You hardly said two words to her the day she installed the bookcases."

"Look, although I wanted to I didn't think I should explore my feelings for her, especially since I was legally married to someone else. I'm sure I've hurt Kelly's feelings, but I don't know how I could've avoided it. If I said anything to her at all, I was afraid she'd be able to tell how I felt about her and that could've been a bad move. Besides, how in the world could the whole thing work out?"

"What work out? I'm not sure what you're referring to."

Andi looked away, reached for her wine, and sat forward on the sofa, staring into the fire. She took a deep breath. "You know, it's the whole 'I'm here, she's there' thing. I own the gallery here, and she's got her business there. My whole life has been centered here, while hers has always been there. It'd never work."

Elise reached over and began slowly stroking Andi's back as she had when she was a child. "Well, no, it wouldn't if you look at it that way. I was going to suggest that you contact Kelly and at least wish her a Merry Christmas. Although, if you're feeling like that, perhaps she isn't the one for you and you should leave things alone."

Andi glanced over at her aunt, then back at the fire. "Really? That's interesting, coming from you. I thought you were trying to throw us together."

"Sweetie, I was hoping you'd find a friend. At the time I met her, Kelly seemed like a nice woman about your age, that's all. I wasn't trying to set you up with someone else, honestly." Elise leaned around to attempt eye contact and smiled.

Andi took a little sip of wine, and sat back against the sofa again as her lips struggled to keep a full grin from breaking out on her face. "Uh, huh. Sure, you weren't."

Elise looked away, shrugged and took another leisurely sip from her goblet. She gazed back at Andi. "I honestly wasn't. I was thinking more like friend material for you. Once the two of you started spending time together, you perked up considerably. You smiled a lot more and you seemed happier than I've seen you in quite a while."

"I'll admit that being around her and her friends I felt a lot happier than I had for a long time."

"After you left, Kelly seemed very subdued. She asked about you the first couple of times I had her over for lunch. After that, she stopped asking and didn't mention your name again. It took her a while to start acting like herself." She tilted her head as she regarded Andi. "Maybe she feels more for you than you think she does."

Andi looked back at the fire.

"Anyway," Elise sipped her wine, "I guess that doesn't matter if you don't feel the same way about her. Besides, as you said, there's the whole 'you're here and she's there' thing going on."

"I don't know what to do." Andi's gaze didn't move from the fire, her reply so quiet Elise almost didn't hear it.

"What do you want to do? I mean if there wasn't the distance thing going on, what would you like to do?"

"Tell you the truth, that evening we spent with Shawn and Carrie was the most relaxed and fun evening I've had in a very long time. I realized early on that Kelly and I seemed to be good together. At the same time, all I could think of was that I didn't have the right to feel anything at all for her. I'm still married, after all."

"What, you can't have friends? Is that what Jo tried to make you feel? Like you aren't allowed to have any fun or friends without her?"

"Well, sort of. Maybe. I don't know. I'm not sure now what Jo did and what I put on myself."

Elise set her glass back down on the coffee table and put her arm around Andi. Andi snuggled into her aunt's embrace, her head on her shoulder, as her gaze lingered on the fire.

"Look, my dear, if you care at all about Kelly, and I'm pretty sure you do, why don't you call or text her and at least give her a clue what's going on, even if you don't want to go into details. She probably thinks by now that you don't care about her in the slightest."

"I know that. Saying goodbye would've been hard and I might've given away or told her how I felt about her. Like I said, I'm still married. I'm also afraid if Jo thinks I have someone else in my life that she'll make things hard for me, even though the divorce was her idea and she had already moved on to someone else while we were together. I bought that gallery during our relationship, even if it was before we were married. She made an appearance occasionally for showings, but I made it what it is. I'm still afraid of losing it, or at least half of it, to her."

"You're divorcing. Jo has enough money and property of her own. You don't owe her anything, although I can understand your concern. Remember, Jo's the one that hurt you. I don't see Kelly doing the same thing. I do agree with you that being apart for a while might be good for both you and Kelly. Maybe your concern that Jo might go after the gallery in retribution is valid. If that's truly a possibility, perhaps having no contact with Kelly might be better for now. However, I wouldn't leave Kelly in the dark for very long. She might be hurt enough that she won't want to be your friend again, let alone more than that later."

"I know. I'm thinking now that I'd like it if you could make those phone calls you offered earlier. I'd love anything that could speed up the process and give me my life back as soon as possible."

Chapter Twenty

CARRIE HANDED KELLY ANOTHER Christmas cookie, this one shaped like a star with green icing and little snowflakes on it. Kelly had a sudden thought that they should make Christmas cookies in the shapes of palm trees and flamingos there in Florida.

"Thanks, Carrie. As usual, dinner was great and these cookies are outstanding." She bit off a part of her star cookie. "Thanks for inviting us."

"You're always welcome. You know that."

"You're family, Kelly. Remember that," Shawn said.

"Does that mean you're adopting me?" Kelly chuckled.

"Not on your life," Carrie said. "We were hoping that you'd be here with someone special in your life this year."

"I do have someone special." Kelly looked over at Piper, asleep on her cushion in the corner by the fireplace.

"I was referring to the two-legged variety, actually. Piper's a real sweetie, but..."

"Yeah, well, so far, it ain't happenin'." Kelly let out a small sigh. "Although Piper's very special in her own way, I haven't given up hope of finding that human someone special. At least, not yet. In the meantime, I'm not holding my breath."

"So...what happened to Andi, anyway? Haven't you heard anything at all from her?" Shawn asked.

"Nah." Kelly took another bite of cookie. "Other than something about 'nice job' the day I installed the bookcases, I haven't heard one word. Not even a text message saying Merry Christmas or anything. How 'bout we leave it at that."

"Okay, I know you've seen Elise since she left, haven't you? Hasn't she mentioned Andi at all?" Carrie asked.

Kelly studied the ceiling before looking back at Carrie. "Look, the last time I saw Elise was before she went back to New York for Christmas. She had me over for lunch a couple of times after I finished the bookcases. We didn't talk about Andi. Can we leave this alone?"

"Sorry, we just wondered what happened. If you don't want to talk about it, that's fine with us." Carrie stood to get the coffee carafe from the kitchen table. "We liked her. I got the impression she liked you, too."

"If someone takes off without saying a word and hasn't said a word since, I'd say she didn't like me as much as she let on." Kelly got up and walked to the window, her back to them.

"Maybe, maybe not," Shawn said. "Is it possible she's got some good reason? I mean I ran all the way to Atlanta to try to figure things out."

"Yes, you did. You, however, didn't run off without saying anything."

"I was going to. That was my original plan, simply to get away from the situation. If Carrie hadn't called me that night and invited me over, I wouldn't have told her I was leaving. My weakness for chocolate pie did me in. Sounds awful, doesn't it?"

"It was awful after you took off," Carrie said, back with the coffee carafe. "As I recall, you did call me while you were gone. You didn't leave me in the dark completely."

"So possibly you need to call Andi," Shawn suggested. "If nothing else, tell her you were thinking about her and wanted to wish her a Merry Christmas."

"Look, she's the one that took off, not me. I tried to call her twice and left her a message each time. There was no call back or even a text. Don't you think she should be the one that calls? Seems to me that she's made it clear she doesn't want any contact from me."

"Not necessarily. Maybe she...oh, I don't know. Now I'm running out of 'maybe she's' for you," Shawn said.

Kelly turned around, put her hands in her pockets and looked at the two of them. "There's something else I didn't tell you. Elise sort of warned me about getting hung up on Andi."

"Really? Her aunt did that? Why?" Carrie asked.

"Elise was concerned that I might be getting too attached to Andi. She told me it was good of me to be her friend, but she warned me not to expect anything else from her. Since Andi sure left in a hurry, I guess Elise was right."

"Again, not necessarily. She seemed very happy in your company," Carrie said.

"Right, happy enough to want me to kiss her." Kelly suddenly wished she hadn't said that.

"She wanted you to kiss her? Really? When?" Shawn asked.

"I shouldn't have told you that."

"Too late now. You already did. Give." Shawn leaned forward in her chair. Carrie looked over at her with a look that said leave it alone. "Hey, it's not me this time!"

Carrie rolled her eyes and shook her head. "Kelly, you don't have to tell us anything you're uncomfortable with."

"Oh, I might as well." Kelly sat back down, reached for her coffee, and took a sip. "We drove out to Fort Myers Beach that night we had dinner with you guys. We were sitting there looking at the water and the moon. She seemed chilly and moved over very close to me, so I put my arm around her."

"Uh huh...and?" Shawn prompted. Carrie rolled her eyes at Shawn and shook her head.

"The next thing I remember is her looking up at me with those big beautiful brown eyes. I wanted to kiss her and it was clear she wanted me to...so I kissed her. It wasn't a big deal kiss, simply a little kiss."

Carrie smiled. "Then what?"

"Then she gave me a cute smile and snuggled in closer, but that's it. We left soon after that."

"That sounds fairly innocent," Carrie said.

"Nothing was said about it?" Shawn asked.

"Well, later I did say something about how I shouldn't have kissed her, since she's my friend and all. She said in so many words that it was no big deal and that was that. Nothing else was said about it. Shortly before she got in her car to leave that night, she kissed me on the cheek. The next day she took off for New York without saying goodbye."

They all sat there in silence. The clock ticked from its spot on the mantle and the fire crackled in the fireplace.

"Is it possible that you're more than a friend to her, and although she enjoyed that kiss she wasn't ready for it? I mean, she recently broke up with someone, right?" Carrie took a sip of her coffee.

"I guess anything's possible. She could've said goodbye, though, even if it was only a text message saying 'gotta run, thanks for the nice evening.' She didn't even tell me she was leaving. As I said, I tried to call her and even left a message. She didn't pick up and she never returned my call, so I'd say it's obvious that she doesn't want any contact from this end. Again, that doesn't sound like someone who cares much about me."

"Then again," Carrie said, "it could be because she does care for you. All I'm saying is, things aren't always how they seem on the surface."

"What am I supposed to do? Sit around and wait for her to come back or call or something?"

"No, I'm not saying that. Like someone wise once told me, don't give up on her yet." Carrie smiled. "On the other hand, you don't have to sit at home and wait for her, either."

"Yeah, I know. I know I shouldn't have started caring about her. I knew she had a life in New York that I wouldn't want to be part of. I'm not the society type."

"No, you're not. You do clean up well, however." Shawn laughed and wiggled her eyebrows.

"Very funny." Kelly showed a small grin. "I do, don't I?" She grinned bigger.

Carrie laughed. "Of course, you do. You looked great at our wedding. I'm surprised some woman didn't swoon right there." She put her hand to her forehead in a dramatic show.

"Swoon. That's a good one. Wow, you two are full of it this evening. Seriously, it's possible Andi decided it'd be better that we not have any contact because it wouldn't work. Who knows? Whatever it is, I guess I'd better get over it."

Shawn thought for a second. "You and Andi enjoyed each other's company while she was here. It could be that's all it was supposed to be."

"True. I do like Elise, though. She wants to stay friends with me, as well as keep me around for future jobs. Andi's part of her life, so I need to let it go, I guess."

"Hard as that sounds, yes, that seems like a good idea. At least for now," Carrie said. "As I said earlier, if I were you I wouldn't rule her out completely as a friend, anyway. You might be surprised down the road."

"What do you mean?"

"I mean that situations change and people change. Just sayin'."

"I think I'm getting tired of always being the one left standing on the sidelines, as far as love is concerned. I pretty much knew Andi wasn't ready for anything more than being friends. Too bad that it didn't stop me from caring about her more than I knew I should've. That's my fault."

"So, now what? You can't turn it off like a water spigot. She must have a clue that you care about her. I mean, that kiss..." Shawn said.

"Right. That kiss...clearly it didn't mean much to her if she can take off like that without a word. I know I wouldn't have. I was a bit concerned about it."

"Did you say something to her afterward about it? Like it was nothing or something?" Carrie asked her.

"All that was said was that it was a spur of the moment thing on both our sides. And that we're friends still. Maybe I should've let it be? Did I do something wrong again?" Kelly stood up once more and began pacing the room.

"I doubt you did anything wrong at all. This whole thing is mostly that you have no idea what's happening because she took off like that. She left without leaving you a clue. She could've at least sent you a text." Shawn said.

"Yes, she could've done that. It would've taken only a few seconds and I wouldn't be wondering what's going on," Kelly said. "Or maybe I would. Who knows?" She sat back down.

"Kelly, you know we love you. We think you're one of the most loving, giving people in the world." Carrie reached over and patted Kelly's leg.

"Thanks. Why do I sense there's more you want to say?"

"Because there is?" Carrie grinned. "I wonder if it's possible that she figures you'll still be around after she gets back. Maybe you shouldn't be so available when that happens. Maybe you need to let her know you aren't just sitting around waiting for her to come back...and maybe you need to keep yourself out there for now. I can almost guarantee you that she isn't simply sitting at home thinking about you."

"Probably not. She has her friends there and the gallery, so she's got plenty to do. Besides, how do I know she didn't go running back to her ex? That could be why I haven't heard anything from her."

"Haven't you talked to Elise about her at all?" Carrie asked.

"Not really. Not since right after Andi left. Haven't had a reason to bring her up since then. Plus, I haven't talked to Elise since she went back to New York."

"Oh."

"Yes, she said she always goes back to the city for the Christmas holiday. She told me she'd really miss it if she couldn't."

"Hmm, I'd bet you ten bucks that Andi's spending at least part of Christmas with her, since they're so close. Especially Christmas Day. What do you think?" Shawn said.

"Are you thinking I should call Elise and wish her a Merry Christmas and see if she says anything about Andi?" Kelly looked pointedly at

Shawn. When Shawn grinned, Kelly did, too. "Well, I should have, anyway, so there's nothing strange about that. Good idea, there, Shawn. In fact, that's a great idea."

"Sometimes I have a good one."

"Yeah, once in a while. I should shove off, then." Kelly stood up and whistled for Piper, who lazily began stretching. "I'll give Elise a call this evening," Kelly said. "Thanks again for inviting me over for dinner. You made my Christmas much nicer."

"And you made ours perfect. Thanks for coming." Carrie hugged Kelly. "You know we love you."

"Yeah, and I love you guys, too." Kelly reached for the door, Piper fast on her heels. "You know, this time two years ago you were barely engaged. Now here you are an old married couple." She laughed. "Merry Christmas you two. Here's to many more wonderful Christmases together."

Kelly opened the Durango door and Piper jumped in and hopped onto the passenger seat. Kelly paused a second before turning the key to start it. She could've sworn she heard someone say her name just then. And she could have sworn it was Andi.

***

As soon as Kelly got home, she plopped down on the sofa and dialed Elise before she could chicken out. In two rings, Elise answered.

"Merry Christmas, Kelly! What a delightful surprise." Elise's cheery voice on the other end made her relax immediately.

"And Merry Christmas to you, too. I wanted to call and wish you the same. I saw all the snow there in New York on the news and thought of you. I assume you're all warm and cozy holed up in your apartment during the storm."

"Thanks for thinking of me. And yes, I'm all warm and cozy here. I have a lovely fire in the fireplace, too. Did you have a good Christmas?"

"Oh, yes. I just got back from a great dinner with my friends Shawn and Carrie. They're the ones I took Andi to meet while she was here. Anyway, we had a great time and I ate too many Christmas cookies. How about you? Did you have a nice Christmas, too?"

"Yes, I did. Andi was here, as usual. In fact, she left only a few minutes ago."

"That's nice. I'm sure you had a wonderful day together. How is she, by the way?" Kelly hoped she slid that question in casually.

"She's fine. Working hard at the gallery and all. She's got a lot on her plate right now, so she's staying busy. How about you? Are you staying out of trouble?" Elise laughed.

"Oh, yeah, you know me. I rescue the damsels. I don't get into trouble myself. At least not much..." Kelly laughed. "Well, I don't want to keep you. I wanted to wish you a Merry Christmas. Oh, and if you need help with all those books and things after you get them down here, let me know. I'll be glad to help. I'm great at grunt work."

"Well, thanks! I might take you up on that...Kelly—"

"I better go. Listen, when you see Andi again, tell her I said hi. Be sure to let me know if you need help with the books and all. Merry Christmas!"

Kelly hung up before Elise could say anything else. From the tone of Elise's voice, Kelly figured she didn't want to hear what was coming next about Andi.

Chapter Twenty-one

VALENTINE'S DAY HAD COME and gone. Spring was on its way in southwest Florida, meaning the rainy season was around the corner. For now, the skies were blue, the birds were singing, it was warm during the day, and there was no doubt in anyone's mind why so many snowbirds were still there and wouldn't leave till the beginning of May.

Yesterday, Elise had called Kelly to ask for help unpacking and invite her to stay for lunch. There were boxes filled with books, all needing a home on the shelves. Kelly had agreed and now she was once again turning into Elise's driveway.

There was another car in the circular driveway. Elise hadn't mentioned anyone else being there. Perhaps she had recruited another friend to help unpack the boxes. She pulled into place beside the cute little red Subaru Crosstrek.

She knocked on the front door. While she waited for someone to answer, she looked back at the driveway to check out the car again. As the door opened, she looked back. It was not Elise standing there, it was Andi. Her hair was longer and sat on her shoulders in waves. Other than that, she looked exactly as Kelly remembered. Kelly's mouth started to go dry as her stomach rolled over. Although her legs prepared to make a U turn, run to the car, and leave, her feet betrayed her by keeping her rooted to the spot. Seconds ticked by as they locked eyes. Kelly forced herself to glance back toward the driveway, breaking their eye contact, as she took a breath. "I'm here to help Elise with her books."

Andi waved Kelly into the house. "Hi, Kelly. Aunt Elise is in her office. You know where that is, so I'll let you show yourself back. I'll be in in a few minutes. Can I get you something to drink? We have Pepsi, iced tea, and ice water."

"Thanks, a Pepsi would be great." Kelly followed her into the kitchen. "How've you been?"

"Fine, and you?" Andi asked as she handed Kelly the bottle of soda and placed a second one on the counter.

"I'm good. Well, I'll go see what Elise is up to, then." Kelly twisted off the cap and lifted the soda bottle in salute. "Thanks."

***

Andi watched Kelly's back as she walked down the hall toward Elise's office. She hadn't realized how seeing Kelly again would make her feel. The minute she saw her standing in the doorway, she was so glad to see her she wanted to throw her arms around her and hug her close. She couldn't, not after all those months of nothing. She forced herself to remain motionless. She'd have been devastated if Kelly pushed her away. Her throat had nearly closed and she had a hard time even saying hello to her without it coming out as a squeak. Instead, she fell back to sounding business-like, which might not have been such a good idea.

Kelly's cool attitude toward her was all her own fault. Deep down inside, she knew it. *What if Kelly doesn't care for me anymore? Leaving like I did could've killed whatever we might've had. If so, I can't blame her. That's all on me. Or I could've been wrong about the whole thing and she was just being nice to me. Now that my divorce is final and I can pursue my life as I choose, I know I want Kelly. It's time to find out if she wants me.*

She stared at her hands again, realizing she was clutching the Pepsi bottle like a lifeline. She knew she had to talk to Kelly. Placing the bottle on the counter, she rubbed her hands together, as if to warm them. *What if Kelly doesn't want to talk to me? What if she has decided the poor little rich girl could just go...? Well, that wasn't a nice thought, but I must face the possibility that it could be exactly that.*

Lunch was almost ready. Andi picked up her soda bottle again and took a sip as she wandered down the hall to Elise's office. As she walked through the door, she could see how animated Kelly was, talking to Elise about building the bookcases. Her aunt was equally animated, clearly excited about how great her office looked now, as they placed Elise's books and other things on the shelves. Even as they opened the boxes, Elise was practically dancing around.

"You know, it looks even nicer in here than I'd originally envisioned it. I have no idea how you come up with your designs for things. All I can say is that you're a genius." Elise opened another box of books.

Kelly was blushing. Andi smiled, finding that quite endearing.

"Thanks," Kelly said. "I enjoy the design part of making things almost as much as the building part. It's great to see someone enjoy what I make as much as I enjoyed making it. I hope you continue to be happy with them for a long time."

"Oh, believe me, I will. I've already called Gladstone to tell Carrie I'm glad they sent you to me."

Quietly, Andi said, "I am, too."

"Thanks," Kelly said, keeping her eyes on Elise. "It was my pleasure. I've made a new friend as well, Elise. You're an easy person to work for."

Andi watched this and realized Kelly was not referring to her. In fact, she seemed to be ignoring her. She hid the tears that began to sting her eyes by taking a sip from her soda again. She decided the next thing to do was to finish making their meal. Lunch she was good at, so she would go back to the kitchen and finish making it, then get through the rest of Kelly's visit the best she could.

She watched Kelly and her aunt chatting away like old buddies, with Elise showing Kelly the various awards she had received over the years and some of her favorite books as they placed the treasured items on the shelves. Kelly appeared to be genuinely interested, not simply humoring her. Andi knew in her heart that Kelly was as sweet as she seemed. None of it was an act. She was herself all the time. So why was Andi feeling shut out of the conversation? It was her. She'd done it to herself. She had shut herself out by sitting there like a lump.

"So, is anyone getting hungry?" Andi asked them.

"I sure am. Another half hour and I think we'll be ready," Elise said.

"Great. Give me about ten minutes heads-up to finish everything, then come on out to the lanai." Andi headed down the hall to the kitchen. As she told herself before, lunch she could do.

***

They had a pleasant meal with ordinary chitchat during which Andi's whereabouts for the last few months wasn't mentioned. The conversation stayed on topics of Elise's office, her bookcases, and the weather, of course. Everyone in Florida talks about the weather. As the conversation waned, Kelly stood, thanked the women for lunch and prepared to leave.

"Thanks again for coming and putting things up on the high shelves for me. I'm not extremely fond of ladders." Elise gave Kelly a hug, leaving one arm around her as she waved the other one to include the whole office. "This is marvelous! I'm literally ecstatic about how my office looks now. I'm going to love working in there all the time."

"Does that mean you're planning to move here shortly?" Kelly asked.

"It's definitely in the works. I merely have to execute the plan," Elise said, grinning at Kelly. "I'm sure now it won't be long. It helps a lot knowing I have this lovely office to work in, with all my things here. Those bookcases made all the difference in the world."

"I'm glad I could make that happen for you. It was a great project."

Andi hung back, watching. "Thanks for coming to lunch."

"Thanks for making such a delicious meal and inviting me." Kelly made every effort to avoid looking directly at Andi for more than a brief glance. Trying not to run, she quickly got into the Durango and wasted no time starting the engine and leaving.

Kelly realized that she'd been almost holding her breath since she saw Andi at the front door. As she pulled out of Elise's driveway, she let out a long sigh and shook her head. Andi could still do it to her, simply by standing there. Yep, she still had a thing for Andi. Unfortunately, it seemed abundantly clear Andi didn't feel the same about her.

As she drove, she thought back to the fun evenings having pie and coffee, the dinner with Shawn and Carrie, and the kiss on the beach. Maybe that was only Andi having fun. She couldn't go on caring for and being around Andi. Today, she'd clearly demonstrated that she no longer cared about her. For her own good, it was finally time to cut the ties. The next time Elise invited her for lunch, she'd make sure Andi wouldn't be there. *At least that's the plan right now.*

***

As Kelly reached the end of Elise's driveway and turned onto the street, Andi made a sudden decision to run out and flag her down to talk to her. Kelly apparently didn't see her, though, and drove away. Andi felt the tears begin to sting her eyes again as she ran back into the house, past Elise standing by the door with her mouth open, and straight to her room. She threw the door shut, sat down on her bed, then lay on her stomach and began sobbing her heart out into her pillow.

She felt silly and heartsick at the same time. *I'm acting like some brokenhearted teenager, heartsick that Kelly might never care for me again.* Despite how foolish she felt, she let herself sob into her pillow until she gave herself a headache.

Chapter Twenty-two

ANDI HEARD HER AUNT knock softly on her bedroom door before opening it.

"Oh, sweetie, is there anything I can do?" Elise sat on the bed beside her and stroked her back softly. "I feel awful for you."

"It's all my fault." Andi sat up and reached for a tissue to dry her reddened eyes. "I shouldn't have cut her out of what was going on. I should've trusted her and told her how I was feeling about her and why I had to go back."

"Maybe it isn't too late. Unless I'm mistaken, Kelly still cares about you. I saw how she looked as you walked into the room. I definitely saw something there. She might've acted like she did because you hurt her feelings. Think about how long it's been since you had contact with her."

"I did what I thought I had to," Andi said, wiping her eyes. "At my age, you'd think I'd know better. I feel like I'm back in junior high or something, instead of being old enough to have kids in junior high. Good grief."

Elise laughed softly. "I think everyone acts like a teenager when love's involved. I still say it might not be too late. If you really care for Kelly, you should call her, go see her if she's willing, and explain the whole thing."

"I'm not sure I should do that. I don't only want Kelly as a friend again. I want to see if we have a chance for more than that. I'm not looking for pity for the poor girl who was going through a breakup. That night at Shawn and Carrie's, I saw what a wonderful relationship they have and I realized I want that. I knew then that I could have that with Kelly if I gave it a chance. Thanks to what I did, it might not be possible anymore."

"There's only one way to know...call her. What's the worst thing that could happen? You can't be any worse off or more miserable than you are right now, right?"

Andi looked at her. "That's probably true."

"Call Kelly and talk to her. She's not a mean person, so she'll probably agree to hear your side of the story. And once you get a chance to explain it all to her, she might accept your apology for your lack of communication. I'm assuming you are planning to apologize, right?"

"Of course, I am. I owe her that much. The way things were today, though, I doubt she's ready to listen to an apology from me. She seemed like she was in a big hurry to get away after lunch."

"I have a feeling she'll listen, at least. If given a chance you two could start over again on a different footing. This time you're both single and it's a whole new ball game."

"Aunt Elise, you always know what to say. You've been right there every time anything happened to me my whole life." Andi sighed. "And here I am, pushing forty hard, and you're still there saying the right things. What would I do without you?"

"I already told you that I plan to live forever, right?" Elise laughed and wrapped her arms around Andi even tighter. "I'd love to see you with a partner you love and who loves you in return like you deserve. I think Kelly could be that someone, if you let her."

Chapter Twenty-three

KELLY'S PHONE RANG. SEEING Andi's number in the display window made her stomach clench, so she let it go to voicemail. Less than a minute later, the message notification dinged. She debated whether to listen to it or delete it. She decided to listen.

Andi's voice was almost a whisper. "Hi Kelly. We didn't get a chance to talk today and I'd like to explain to you what's been going on. I'd also like to ask you to forgive me for being a bit of an idiot. No, I was a complete idiot for not even saying goodbye before I left last year. Please call me."

Kelly listened to the message twice. She couldn't believe this. *What could Andi possibly want from me now?* She hit the delete button on the message and tossed the phone onto the sofa table. She sat there for a few minutes, staring into space. *Should I call her back? Maybe I should face her and put an end to it all. Or what if Andi does have an explanation worth hearing?* As she reached for her phone to punch in Andi's number, her phone rang again. It was Andi, again. She picked up.

"Kelly, I'd like to talk to you in person. I need to explain some things to you and we didn't get any time to talk while you were here today."

"That's okay. There isn't much to say. After all, we haven't talked in months. You've been busy, I've been busy. I don't think there's much to talk about."

"That's not all. There's more. Can we have coffee somewhere and talk for a bit so I can tell you about it in person...like we used to?"

"Look, there really isn't—"

"Please," Andi pleaded.

A deafening silence hung between them until Kelly sighed. "Look, I don't know what you want from me. Things have changed and it's not the same now."

"I know it isn't. I also know it's all my fault. If you don't want to see me again after we talk, well, I'll understand and accept that. Please, can I just have a few minutes of your time?"

"All right. Why don't you come over here? We can have coffee while you talk and I listen."

"When?"

"How about now?"

"Now? Okay, give me a few minutes and I'll be right over. Thank you."

As Kelly spooned coffee into the coffeemaker she shook her head, wondering what in the world Andi could possibly have to say to her. She steeled herself for what could be coming. *Andi could have gone back to her ex and wants to explain that to me in person. Or she realized that a relationship is out of the question and wants us to be friends. Or...what? Who knows? Maybe having Andi come here wasn't such a great idea. Meeting on my own turf where we could talk in private seemed like a good idea as I said it. I hope that wasn't a mistake. The only thing I can do to protect myself is to keep my distance, both physically and emotionally. The table in the kitchen nook will take care of the physical part. The emotional part will be a lot harder.*

There was a timid knock on the door. Kelly opened it and there stood Andi—her eyes a bit red like she might've been crying. *Oh, great.* It was difficult for Kelly to avoid reacting visibly to the sight of her. Her heart beat a little harder as she stepped aside and motioned for Andi to come in. She didn't say anything as she shut the door behind Andi and turned for the kitchen.

Andi stood wringing her hands. "Thanks for inviting me over. I'm sure this wasn't easy for you. You should know this isn't exactly comfortable for me, either."

"Have a seat," Kelly said. She motioned for Andi to sit at the dinette table as she fetched two mugs of coffee and the cream and sugar.

Kelly sat down, looking at Andi. She waited while Andi kept staring at her coffee mug. "I'm listening."

Andi took a sip of her coffee and swallowed hard. "I was married," she blurted out.

"What? When?" Kelly's eyes widened, she looked out the window for a second, then her head snapped back to look at Andi, her brows furrowed. "Wait, you said 'was married,' didn't you?"

"Yes. I did. I'm now divorced."

"Wow! You were married while you were here before?"

"I was. I came down here thinking the time away would be good and she'd miss me. I'm ready to tell you what happened now, if you want to hear the whole sordid story."

"If you want to tell me, I'll listen." Kelly picked up her mug and leaned back against the bench as she took a sip of coffee. "Go ahead."

Andi looked down at her own mug, then back up at Kelly. "I fell in love with Jo when she came into a gallery I was working in several years ago, back before I bought it out and made it what it is now. Jo's an artist. You may have heard of her, JoAnne Duncan."

"Actually, I have heard of her. Duncan's picture is in *People* magazine almost as often as Ellen DeGeneres. Unfortunately, she's as infamous for her womanizing as she's famous for her paintings and sculptures. No one would've guessed she was in a relationship."

"Almost everyone has heard of her. She wasn't only in a relationship with me, we were married. I know I shouldn't have married her, knowing what she was like. I fell completely in love and I thought being married might make her settle down. After all, it was Jo who proposed."

"It's hard to believe someone like that would propose marriage to anyone. I'm even more surprised your wedding wasn't highly publicized, like everything else she does."

"We kept it low key, believe it or not. It was a courthouse thing in Pennsylvania. To this day, I've no idea why she wanted to marry me. She still treated me the same way as before; unfortunately, after the wedding we were legally bound."

"Then why in the world did you stay with her? What could've possibly made you want to be treated like that?"

"I still loved her," Andi said in a near whisper, looking down at her cup before looking up into Kelly's eyes. "It took a while before I finally realized that Jo's kind of love wasn't what I wanted or needed any more. I told her I was leaving and I came down to Florida to stay with Aunt Elise while I sorted out in my head what to do next. At first, I thought physical distance would be enough for me to see the situation more clearly. I'm sure now that there was a part of me that thought that possibly Jo and I could work things out. That maybe she'd realize she wanted me."

"I'm sorry. I knew you were going through a bad situation." Kelly shook her head. "It's obvious now that it was much worse than you let on."

"I guess I thought on some level that it was sort of a trial separation to try to get her attention. It turned into a permanent separation right after I met you. I guess I hoped she'd miss me and come running. I thought she'd at least call me and try to get me back. She didn't."

"She didn't contact you at all?"

"Only to text me that she wanted a divorce."

"That's really cold."

"There's more. Aunt Elise didn't know anything about us being married. I hid it from her. That should've said something about the relationship, huh?"

"I'd say so." Kelly took a sip of her coffee. "I'm sorry you had to go through all that. You deserve better. Why did you go back suddenly like you did?"

Andi put her mug down and crossed her arms, leaning against them on the table. "Look, I like you a lot. I was afraid if I stayed any longer that I'd want to do something I didn't feel I had the right to do. I shouldn't have kissed you that night on the beach. Had you kissed me again, I'd have wanted more from you than that little kiss. I could tell. And I didn't have the right to drag you into that whole divorce situation."

"You know what? I would've been fine with being there for you. At least you could've told me what was going on. Instead, you let me think you'd decided to run back to New York and had kicked me to the curb."

"Look, I'm really, really sorry I did that to you." Andi reached across the table and gently placed her hand on Kelly's. She looked up into Kelly's eyes. "You have no idea how sorry I am. At the time, I thought it was the right thing to do. I thought it was the only thing to do. I wanted to be free to come back and see if we had a chance together. I guess, at the time, I wasn't thinking that there might be nothing to come back to because of what I did."

Kelly withdrew her hand. "I pretty much gave up on you. You didn't even return a text message. You don't do that to a friend, Andi. What actually made the sudden exit necessary?"

"Like I said, I'd originally hoped Jo would come around and realize that she truly loved me. Instead, Jo texted me that she wanted a divorce. It happened while I was talking to you about setting up the coffee and dessert thing for the three of us...me, you and Aunt Elise, I mean. We never did do that. I can't remember why."

"Now I understand. That explains why you sounded funny. I wondered what happened. You seemed fine and suddenly you seemed 'not fine.' It was clear you didn't want to talk about it. Why didn't you tell me?"

"To tell you the truth, I felt that I would've had to tell Aunt Elise the truth as well. I'd hidden our marriage from her. She only knew that we were living together in a relationship, and she wasn't thrilled about that. She didn't care for Jo at all."

"I don't blame her, if Jo wasn't treating you well."

"She didn't know Jo and I had problems. No one did. We kept it all lovey in front of others and almost everyone we knew thought we had this perfect life. Of course, by then, most of 'our' friends were her friends. She'd managed to get me to cut myself off from most of my own."

"Then what made Elise dislike Jo? I mean, it seems to me she'd like anyone who made you happy, if you seemed happy to her."

"One would think so. I don't know why, but Aunt Elise never liked her from day one. Every time I tried to pin her down on why she felt like she did, she'd say she didn't know exactly. She just didn't care for her. She invited us over for dinner and holidays and was friendly enough to her. I don't think I could describe her demeanor as warm, though. She isn't into being a phony."

"I gather she isn't. I like Elise. She's quite an interesting woman."

"She likes you, too. She's said so on several occasions." Andi smiled. "And now, every time she looks at those new bookcases, she just smiles. I think she likes you even more every time she sees them."

"Ah, there's that smile I liked to see. Elise does seem to be a good judge of character, as it turns out, at least in your case. So, where do you stand with her? Now that your divorce is final, does she know you were married?"

"Yes, finally, officially, I'm a free woman. I broke down and told Aunt Elise at Christmas. She knew people who knew people and my divorce got fast-tracked. She's very happy that whole thing's over, and so am I."

"Well, that's good. So, what's next?"

"I'm relieved to say that Aunt Elise doesn't have any issue with us being friends," Andi said, looking back into Kelly's eyes. "Or more than friends, for that matter."

"Oh, really?" Kelly frowned. "And what makes you or Elise think I might be interested in still being friends with you or more than that, either, after you left me high and dry for all these months. You have to admit that wasn't at all a polite thing to do."

"Again, you have no idea how sorry I am that I did that. I didn't know if you even cared for me. And it was better for my divorce to be seen alone and lonely and upset. And that's exactly what they saw."

"You mean, it was easier for you to face your friends without someone like me around, who wouldn't have fit in and would've started the rumor mill going?" Kelly sat back in the bench, her arms crossed and face impassive.

"Absolutely not. That wasn't the idea at all. In the beginning, I was going to try to get my divorce alone, and hide it from Aunt Elise. If I'd told you about it, I would've had to tell her. It would only have been fair. And I didn't want to. I really didn't."

"I still don't understand why you didn't just tell her what was going on. Your aunt loves you very much and would've understood."

"I know this sounds stupid. It's because I'd never hidden anything from her before. Ever. Even as a kid, I couldn't hide anything from her. My marriage was the only thing I'd ever kept from her and I felt awful."

Kelly took a deep breath before nodding in response. "I bet you did." She put her elbows back on the table and reached for her coffee mug.

"I had to tell her that I had married Jo without her knowing about it, and that I was getting a divorce, at the same time. I thought that made me sound like such an idiot and a failure, too."

"One question. How...did you manage to hide it from her? I mean, you live in the same city. You saw each other fairly often. Didn't Jo give it away? She must've been proud of marrying you and told people. Seems like it would've gotten back to her somehow, or you or Jo would've slipped up and let the cat out of the bag."

"First of all, it's New York. Very big city. We were only living together as married for a couple of years. Our routine never changed, we didn't make any big announcement, and our friends were sworn to secrecy to keep it out of the press. In that time, we both went to Aunt Elise's only a few times. Mostly I went alone."

"How come she didn't go, too?"

"Jo always seemed to have a 'thing' to attend." Andi held her fingers in the air like quotation marks. "She'd say it was important for me to spend time with my aunt and I didn't need to go to whatever it was she was attending. She'd say it was simply some boring reception or whatever."

"Uh, huh...I can hear a 'but' coming."

"You're right. The next day, I'd see pictures in the paper of some fundraiser or art show or something and there she'd be," Andi paused as she slowly shook her head, "all dressed up in a tux with a couple of gorgeous women hanging on her."

"And that didn't make you mad? I'd have been livid."

"Of course, I was upset. I went to some of those events, too. Despite my presence, they still hung all over her. They did it with me standing right there. I should've known she was drawing them in. It wasn't just them, it was her, too."

"I'm sorry to say this, but you're probably right. If she had been truly monogamous, she would've been sending out very different energy. Plus, standing there close to you and holding your hand would've sent a very different message as well. I'm guessing that's not what she was doing."

"We always walked in together. Shortly after that, she'd say how she had to work the room for business. And there I'd be, on my own. I know people, obviously, and always had lots of them to talk to. To be honest, I always thought she only brought me occasionally because she thought she had to, never because she wanted to." Andi looked down at her hands. "That's what I told her in my divorce papers."

"And she didn't deny any of it?"

"Nope. In fact, she never said a word. She let the whole thing go through her attorney and mine, and it was over without another word between us. We haven't spoken since I left her. As I told you, she even texted me to say she was filing for divorce."

"I'm sorry. Really. That was very, very cold of her."

"I'm sorry, too. Sorry for several things," Andi said.

"Like what? Doesn't sound like you did anything to be sorry for."

"I'm sorry I got involved with someone who didn't love me, for one. I wasted a lot of time with someone who didn't care about me."

"That happens. I bet it happens a lot. It's how we learn, I guess."

"Maybe, but I'm really sorry I actually married her. With emphasis on the 'really' part."

"Yeah, that pretty much stinks. You definitely made a mistake there."

"I'm very sorry I treated you badly because I was trying to cover up what I'd done." Andi looked at her hands again.

"Are you trying to apologize to me for that?"

"Trying to." Andi looked up with the beginning of a little hopeful smile.

"I'm not sure I'm ready to accept your apology. Just because someone treated you badly doesn't give you the right to do it to someone else. You can't simply walk right back in and pretend that it hasn't been months since you had any contact with me and like you didn't ignore my phone messages and texts."

"I know." The words were barely audible.

"I'm sorry you were treated like you were. That was nasty. I hate to say this, but in a way, you let it happen to you. You could've left her any time. You stayed. It's not like you didn't have any place else to go."

"I know."

"I guess I simply don't understand how someone could kiss me at the beach then a few hours later run off without a word."

"I…"

"For months."

"That was bad."

"You know it was. You made me think it was all a mistake and you were only playing around. I started assuming that you'd gone back to Jo and didn't feel like telling me. So that's what I've had to deal with. That, combined with feeling like I didn't mean anything to you…even as a friend. You'll forgive me if I don't immediately say it's all okay and pretend like nothing happened."

"Of course not. I mean, I know I hurt you. I explained what happened. I'd hoped that you'd understand."

"I understand. I can't quite forgive you for how you treated me yet. It's going to take more than a few minutes sitting here with you. How do I know you aren't just using me?"

"Using you?"

"Look, I didn't mean to feel anything for you other than friendship. Obviously, my heart didn't listen and it happened anyway. Even a friend wouldn't have done what you did. But someone who wanted more than that definitely wouldn't have shut me out without any explanation." Kelly shook her head and got up and began pacing the kitchen. "Really? What did you think I'd feel?"

"I guess I was so caught up in my own misery that I didn't think much about how you were feeling. Again, I'm so sorry. I feel like crap for doing that to you."

"I know you're sorry. I get that. Forgiving you is another thing altogether. I need time to think this over and to see that you really want a relationship with me. I won't just say everything's fine so you can run off and live your life and forget about it. If you really do want to be part of my life, as a friend or otherwise, I need to see that you mean it."

Andi slid out of the booth, stood up next to the table, and took one of Kelly's hands in both of hers. She looked at their hands. "Kelly, I never ever intended to hurt you. Please believe I didn't mean to…" She looked directly into Kelly's eyes. "I won't be around here all the time. I can't right now."

Kelly slowly withdrew her hand. "Look, we can take it slowly and try to reestablish being friends. There's a catch, though. I need to know that you don't plan to take off without a word again."

"I promise I'll never do that to you again. If I must leave in a hurry for some reason, I'll at least text you and let you know what's going on. I'll never purposely avoid your calls or texts. I have no other secrets to hide and I want to prove to you that I want you in my life. If you'll only be my friend, friend it is."

A little tear escaped from Andi's right eye, then sat on her cheek. Kelly resisted the impulse to reach out and brush it away. "How long are you going to be here this time?"

"A couple of weeks. Kind of a 'yay, I'm divorced' vacation. Do you think we could do something together? We never did play miniature golf."

"Let me think about it. I'm tied up tomorrow. The next day is possible. How about I call you and see what we can work out?"

"Do you still have my number?"

"You called me. It's in my phone."

"Oh, yeah. Sorry, brain hiccup." She grinned, a sheepish look. "I guess I'd better go. I'll wait for you to call me." Andi reached for Kelly's hand again and held it. "The next move is yours. If I don't hear from you before I go back, I'll assume you aren't interested. I hope you'll call me. I've missed you and I've thought about you every day since I left."

"I'll call you. Give me a little time to digest what you've told me." Kelly slowly withdrew her hand. She knew she was hurting Andi and she didn't want to. She had to force herself not to grab her and hold her, but this had been too much to take in without thinking about it. No matter how much she wanted to believe her, she couldn't jump back in there until she was positive that Andi meant what she was saying.

"All right, then. I hope we'll talk again soon." Andi turned away slowly and almost trudged to the door.

Nearly at the door, Andi suddenly turned around and ran back to Kelly. She wrapped her arms around her and gave her a quick kiss on the cheek scarcely before the tears started. She let go of Kelly and was out the door in seconds. A few seconds more, and the only indication Andi had ever been there was the second empty coffee mug on the kitchen table.

Chapter Twenty-four

"WHAT HAPPENED?" SHAWN ASKED as Kelly came through the door. "You didn't sound like yourself when you called. Are you alright?"

"I'm not sure." Kelly looked around. "Carrie's at work, right?"

"Yes, she's working a little late today. Why? Did you want to talk to her?"

"Actually, no. This is something I'd rather talk to you alone about."

"No problem. Would you like some iced tea or a soda? Or I could make some coffee, if you'd rather have that."

"I wouldn't mind a soda."

"Okay, then, come on back to the kitchen and let's hear what's going on. What happened?"

Kelly took a deep breath as she followed Shawn to the kitchen. "Well, Andi came back."

Shawn nodded slowly. "Oh..."

"Yeah, and you won't believe the story she told me."

"Well, sit down and let's hear it, then." Shawn reached into the fridge for two cans of Pepsi and handed one to Kelly as they sat down at the kitchen table.

"I told you I was going over to Elise's to help her unpack and put up the books and stuff on her bookcases, right?" Kelly popped open the can and took a sip.

"Right."

"Well, I got there, rang the doorbell, and guess who answered the door."

"No..."

"Yep, Andi."

"That must've been a shocker."

"It was, believe me. Elise knew Andi had ignored me all this time, and it'd be awkward for me to be there at the same time she was. Despite that, she didn't mention that Andi was coming at all."

Shawn shook her head and mouthed wow.

"Anyway, we got through that whole thing, since it was mostly me and Elise doing the work. Andi came in to say she was making lunch and Elise asked me to stay. I tried to come up with some excuse to leave. I couldn't think of any way out that wouldn't hurt Elise's feelings. During lunch with them, I made sure I kept the conversation moving about Elise's office and her books and awards and all that."

"That sounds like a good idea. Then what?"

"As soon as I could without being too obvious, I got out of there. Seriously, I didn't want to see Andi. She was pleasant and all that, acting as if nothing ever happened between us. She just made small talk and chitchat. I could barely look at her."

"Oh, Kelly, I thought maybe you were over her."

"I thought so, too, until I saw her standing there in the doorway."

"When did you hear that story you were talking about?"

"A while after I got home, she called me. I was surprised she still had my number, since she hadn't called or texted in months. I assumed she deleted me as a contact. Who knows, she might have gotten it from Elise. Anyway, she wanted to talk."

"Talk? About what?" Shawn sat back in her chair.

"She said she wanted to meet somewhere so she could explain what happened. She didn't want to tell me over the phone."

"And?"

"I invited her over to my house. I made coffee and we sat in the kitchen nook. It was then she dropped the bomb."

"Which was..."

"She said when we first met she was married."

"What?" Shawn sat upright. "Wow!"

"Yeah, that was my reaction. She said she had married her partner somewhere in Pennsylvania while they were there on vacation. It was a spur of the moment thing. Anyway, she had never told Elise about it, so she said she couldn't tell me. While she was here that first time I met her, her wife texted her saying she wanted a divorce."

"That's one of the crappiest things I've heard of lately. Texting to tell your wife you want a divorce. Wow. Really poor form. I wouldn't even do that to one of my fictional characters." Shawn sat back again.

"I know. Andi was apparently thinking Jo would want her to come back or something if she came down here and got away. After a while she realized that wasn't happening. That text let her know it was finally over. Elise only knew it was a relationship breakup, although that was bad enough. She had no idea, apparently, what was really going on."

"Definitely stinks. Still, why did she run off and ignore you all that time?"

"That's what I asked her. She said she wanted to tell me, however she felt that if she did, she had to tell Elise first. She said she was starting to really care for me, more than as a friend, and was scared. She said she wanted to get her life straightened around first."

"Right, I get that. Yet..."

"Exactly. She could've told me that without going into more detail. She could've done a lot of things that she didn't. Just because Jo was mean to her didn't give her the right to do what she did to me. You don't treat a friend that way, let alone someone you're interested in having something more with."

"And you told her all of that, I assume."

"I did. Almost word for word. Geez, she looked all sorry and all that. She said she was sorry several times. Part of me thinks she merely wants forgiveness so she can move on with her life. Even now, I'm not completely sure what she wants."

"I bet." A slow grin spread from Shawn's lips to her eyes.

"What? What's so funny?" Kelly stood up, crossed her arms, and glared.

"Hey, this time it isn't me. How much time have we spent talking out my woman-problems? It dawned on me that I was glad it wasn't me this time and it won't be me ever again. I'm sorry...I couldn't help myself."

"Oh." Kelly sat back down. "Well, okay, then. Still..."

"I'm sorry. Keep talking."

"I don't know what to do about this situation. I'd like to forgive her, if I can convince myself that she means it. How can I know?"

"I guess I got lucky with Carrie. She didn't make me beg. Then again, I didn't spend several months away without speaking, either."

"Right. There's that. I'd like to believe that she wants to start over and give her another chance. I'm not sure she genuinely wants me. She's still that New York girl who doesn't live here. She could easily meet someone there that's more up her alley."

"What do you mean? You two seem perfect for each other. Plus, her aunt likes you."

"Yes, Elise does like me. Andi made a point of saying how much Elise likes me and how much she didn't like Jo. What I mean is that she could meet someone else in the art world or in her social circle."

"Kelly, I know you don't think of what you do as art. You don't just renovate houses. Believe me, some of your work, especially your woodworking, is as much art as a painting or sculpture. I think that's one of your attractions for her...besides your obvious charms, of course." Shawn chuckled.

"There's that." A little grin caught the edges of Kelly's mouth. "I finally understand how you felt at the time you were trying to deal with your attraction to Carrie after Jen stomped on your heart. Only this time, it's the same woman. I'm not sure that she won't do it again."

"Okay, I'll give you a little advice. Take it slowly. Ask her out for something non-romantic. Lunch would work. Take her someplace that if this doesn't work out it won't be a place you'll go and get a constant reminder of her."

"Like where?"

"Well, first off, don't go someplace you've already been. And don't go someplace you go to a lot on your own, either."

"That makes sense...I know. Cockatoo Cove over on Sanibel. It's a fun place to have lunch and I don't have any connection to it. I've only been there a couple of times and never with a date."

"Good idea. I think I remember that place. It looks kind of like something from a fifties Florida postcard, right?"

"That's the place. I recall it being fun and definitely unromantic."

"Then it sounds perfect. You can eat a pleasant lunch and laugh a bit. Nothing heavy duty at all. It might be a good idea to avoid anything that seems like a real date until you're convinced she's going to be around for more than a few days...at least communication-wise."

"I don't know why I couldn't think of this myself. My brain seems to get a little fogged up whenever I even think about her. Sad, isn't it?"

"Not really. I felt the same way about Carrie. I'm not saying that means that Andi's 'the one.' She could be. There's only one way to find out."

"Yeah, and it could lead to a world of hurt."

"Or..."

"I know."

Chapter Twenty-five

"I THINK YOU'LL LIKE this place," Kelly said to Andi as they pulled into the driveway of Cockatoo Cove.

"I'm sure I will," Andi grinned as she took in the huge white bird on the front of the restaurant.

"I've been here once or twice before. It's a bit kitschy, which is part of its charm."

As they got out of the Durango, they could hear what sounded like parrots in the trees. There weren't any, of course, but the well-hidden speakers made you look up to see if they were there. The building itself was brightly painted in shades of red, blue, yellow, white, and green featuring their namesake cockatoos, along with parrots and pirates. An almost-real looking motion activated cockatoo greeted them as they walked through the door with a squawk and, "Aye, Maties! Welcome to Cockatoo Cove!"

Andi's face lit up and she giggled. Kelly wanted to grab her and hug her tight. Instead, she looked for the hostess and held up two fingers. They were led into the dining area, which had so much stuff hanging from above that you couldn't see the dark-painted ceiling. It gave the impression of being in a jungle, with the noises and vines.

After they were seated and handed menus, they studied the decorations. There were tree trunks to the ceiling, looking for all the world like the building had grown up around them. Looking up, all they could see were vines, fake lizards, stuffed monkeys, along with parrots and cockatoos. The darkened room had a bit of a breeze blowing through it from somewhere, making the vines and leaves rustle and move. The overall feeling was of being outdoors in a jungle at twilight, except with air conditioning.

"This place is delightful," Andi said over her menu. "I had no idea something like this existed. The pirate cove theme is cute and fun, just a little over the top, and I like it."

"Good. The menu items have funny names, too."

"I see that. There's the Pirate's Gold grilled cheese and it goes downhill from there. Hilarious!"

"I thought this would give you a laugh. Try to order your lunch with a straight face, if you can. The waiters probably hear this stuff all day long."

"You mean, I shouldn't say 'argh' like a pirate?" Andi began giggling.

Their waiter arrived, dressed in long, black zig-zagged cut shorts and a red shirt, with a red bandana tied around his head. Oh, and then there was that obviously fake parrot perched on his left shoulder.

"Ahoy there, maties. You can say 'argh' like a pirate if you like, no problem." The waiter's banter made Andi giggle again. "And what can I bring you to eat and drink? Octopus? Grog? Or would you prefer something a bit less adventurous?" He was laughing, obviously enjoying his job.

"Well, I'm not quite that adventurous. Let's see…I think I'll have the Treasure Chest, the club sandwich. What're you having, Kelly?"

"I'll have the Pirate's Gold. I love grilled cheese, and this one has ham and other stuff in it, too. That sounds fun and edible."

The waiter grinned. "Everything on the menu is edible, believe me. I've eaten every item several times over since I started working here. And what can I bring you to drink with those fine choices? We have a good selection of beer and soda, in addition to iced tea and lemonade."

"I'm going with a Pepsi." Andi handed back her menu.

"Me, too." Kelly handed hers back, as well. "What if I had wanted the Grog? What's that?"

"Oh, it's a secret recipe. Want to try it?" He winked at Kelly.

"Um…okay. We'll take one and we can both taste it."

"I'll be right back with one Grog and two Pepsi Colas while your lunch is being prepared." The waiter disappeared and it appeared he might be chuckling.

"It's going to be something gross, isn't it?" Andi asked.

"Probably. I bet they don't get many people asking for it."

"But you did. Aren't you the adventurous one! What made you do that?" Andi leaned forward with her arms on the table.

"I've no idea. Maybe you bring out the playful side of me."

"Then that's good, right?"

"Could be. What are you planning to do with the rest of the time you're here?"

"Actually, I was hoping to be able to spend a lot of it with you. I know you're working, but when you aren't…I want to show you that I do care about you."

"Well, lunch is a start. I'm still feeling skittish about this whole thing. I mean, last time it felt very comfortable hanging out with you and talking and all...then it all fell apart. I don't want to go through that again."

"I don't blame you. I don't want to go through that again, either."

The waiter brought what looked like a pewter drinking mug with a bubbly orangish-brownish looking concoction in it, along with their two sodas. He set the mug in front of Kelly. "Take a sip of the Grog and tell me what you think."

Kelly took the handle of the mug and gingerly brought it to her nose. She sniffed the liquid inside then shrugged. "It doesn't smell gross. Here goes."

She raised the mug to her lips and took a sip. It tasted of root beer and orange soda mixed together. Not nasty, not great, either. She took another sip with Andi and the waiter still looking on expectantly.

"Well?" Andi and the waiter asked simultaneously.

"It's drinkable, although I don't think I'll order it again. Want a sip?" She put the mug down and scooted it toward Andi.

"I'm not sure." She looked into the mug at the liquid inside. "What the heck, you only live once. You're not showing signs of poisoning." Andi laughed and reached for the mug. She took a sip. "Hey, this stuff isn't half bad," she said, taking another sip.

The waiter laughed. "Usually the kids think it's great and drink it right down. The adults are not usually quite as sure about it. Maybe you two are just overgrown kids. Enjoy. I'll be back in a few more minutes with your food."

Andi moved to hand the mug back to Kelly.

"Tell you what, you can keep that Grog stuff if you like. It seemed awfully sweet to me."

Andi shrugged and kept sipping on it.

"How's your gallery doing?" Kelly asked.

"Ah...changing the subject to something else safe. Okay. My gallery's thriving. We had a showing for G. K. Charles, who's a local up and coming photographer. She wasn't known much outside New York, previously. I think her showing in our gallery gave her a beneficial push. She's very talented and she deserves it. On top of that, she has a great personality. She'll do well."

"She's a new friend now?"

"Yes, I think so. We've stayed in touch since her showing ended a couple of weeks ago. I believe she'll get showings in larger galleries soon. I saw some of the acquisitions people for big collectors at our show and they bought a few prints. That will start the ball rolling for her, for sure."

"I didn't know you handled photography. I guess I thought of your gallery having only paintings and sculpture and the like."

"I'll have you know we handle all kinds of art. I like to think that we have an open mind to what can constitute a piece of artwork. You might be especially interested in our woodworking items." She reached into her bag and retrieved her cell. "Here, let me show you. I have a few pictures on my phone." She did several quick taps and flicks on her screen before handing it to Kelly. "If you wave over it from right to left, it will take you to the next one. There should be four or five photos."

Kelly took the phone and looked at the first picture. It was of a modern art type sculpture made from wood. The next one showed a beautiful small chest with a carved lid in the shape of a peacock with the tail feathers all splayed out. The detail was amazing. Next there was a small tripod table. "What made this piece something you would have in your gallery?" She turned the phone around to show Andi.

"That little table is all of one piece of wood. It's basically a useable sculpture. I thought it was something amazing, so we have it. What do you think so far?"

"Interesting." Kelly turned to the last picture. It was of the top of her kitchen table. "What's this? It looks like the table in my kitchen."

"It is. It's not in my gallery, however it would fit right in since it's a real work of art. I took the picture the first time I was at your house. I probably should've asked your permission first, and for that I apologize. I confess I thought it was beautiful and I wanted to remember it."

"I see. And now what do you want?" Kelly handed the phone back to Andi.

"I don't understand." Andi tilted her head, brows furrowed in question.

"Yes, you do. You want something from me and I'm still not sure what it is."

Andi took a deep breath. "Kelly, I want you."

"You want me for what?" She leaned back in her seat, her arms crossed, words soft and measured. "You want me to make another table for your gallery? You want me to make one for you? What? I assume you showed me those pictures for a reason." She shrugged.

Andi sighed heavily and looked into Kelly's eyes. "If you never make another one of those tables or a pretty box like you made for Shawn and Carrie or another rocking chair or even a stair bannister, I still want you. I just want you in my life. The only reason I showed you those pictures was to point out that you truly are an artist. I know you don't think of yourself that way, because I've heard you put yourself down. I see what you don't and your friends can see it. You have a load of talent."

"Right. And you want to sell things that I might make."

"No...I could, don't get me wrong. Like I said, if you never made another piece like those, I still want to be with you."

Their conversation was interrupted by the waiter bringing their food. Each plate was decorated with little pirate flags and swords stuck in each half of their sandwiches. This time, the waiter only asked if they needed anything else, then disappeared.

"Well, it looks good," Andi said.

"Yes, it does. Time to dig in."

The next few minutes were taken up with nodding and thumbs up as they took their first bites. Even the French fries got a thumbs up.

After a few bites, Andi asked, "Are you thinking about what I said?"

"Actually, I was thinking about how good this is. At the same time, I'm pondering what you said." She put her sandwich down and looked at Andi. "I started caring for you a lot when you were here before. I held onto the hope that you felt the same way, even for some time after you left. As hard as it was to let go of that, I pretty much had to. It's been rough having you walk back in after all these months and say you care for me and want me. Even a month after you left, had you done this, I'd have been ecstatic. Even now, there's a part of me that wants to throw caution to the wind and pretend that nothing happened. I can't do that. I just can't yet. I'm still getting used to you being here and it's going to take some time."

Andi nodded slowly. "I understand that."

"Plus, even if there is still some connection between us, there's the whole you're there, I'm here thing...even though I hate to keep repeating it."

"I know. If you're willing, I know we could work that out. I know you're not interested in moving to New York."

"No, I can't. I don't know if there can be anything more than friendship between us with that whole thing going on. I don't think I could do a long-distance relationship. I don't believe they work."

"Well, let's just see how this goes. I'm sure if we can work out the rest of it, we can work out these other issues. Aunt Elise convinced me that nothing is impossible. I have some ideas about how to make it happen." Andi smiled, picked up a French fry, and dredged it through the ketchup on her plate. "I'm willing if you're willing."

Kelly took a deep breath. "I'm willing to try."

After a few bites of her sandwich and some 'this isn't half bad' remarks, Kelly had a thought. "How'd you like to come to my house tomorrow for supper? I'll grill steaks and the fixings, and invite Shawn and Carrie over. I'm sure they'd like to see you again."

Andi looked up at Kelly. "That sounds like fun. I'd love to see them."

Kelly grinned. "All right, then, supper at six it is. Don't bring anything except yourself. We're pretty casual around here, as you probably noticed, so don't dress up any. It's a cookout."

"I'm already looking forward to it. I haven't been to anything like that in a very long time."

"I haven't had a cookout for a long time. In fact, the last time I had one I spilled chocolate ice cream sauce all over Carrie's shorts. Don't wear anything you care about. Just warning you."

On their way, back Andi reached over and patted the back of Kelly's hand that was lying on the center armrest. Without looking, Kelly turned her hand up and Andi put hers in Kelly's. Kelly glanced over with a faint smile, then back to the road. They rode the rest of the way back that way, speaking very little. Once they got back to Elise's to drop Andi off, Andi kissed Kelly's hand, and then reached over and kissed Kelly's cheek.

"I had a great time. Thanks for inviting me. I'll see you tomorrow. If you get bored in the meantime, you know where to find me."

"I had fun being with you, too. See you tomorrow at six."

Kelly drove away and found herself touching the place on her cheek where Andi's lips had touched her. She took a deep breath, letting it out slowly. *Yep, Andi can still do it to me. Can we make this work?* Her brain was going around in circles trying to figure it all out. She had only kissed her once, but she knew she wanted to try.

Chapter Twenty-six

"ALL RIGHT, GIVE! HOW did lunch go?" Shawn barked through the phone.

"It was nice. The food was good. Have you ever tried their Grog?" Kelly laughed, opened the slider to the lanai, and sat on the lanai sofa. Piper jumped up to lie down next to her and put her head on Kelly's thigh.

"That's not what I'm interested in...come on..."

"Well, I'd say it was illuminating." Piper was staring at her, so she scratched her ears.

"Big word. Very little telling."

"Okay, then, she showed me some pictures of some woodworking type art items she has in her gallery. She told me some of what I do could fit right in. That it's really art."

"What, she's back to wanting you to make stuff for her gallery?"

"Nope, she said she was trying to make a point. She said she doesn't care if I ever make anything she could put in the gallery. She just wants to be with me."

"Wow. That's putting it out there."

Kelly patted Piper before standing up and began pacing the room. "Yes, it is. I told her I'm still looking at the whole 'you're there and I'm here' thing. I'm not sure it can work at all. I can't move to New York if we get serious."

"Well, you could, I guess..."

"No, I can't. I'd never fit in. Plus, I love living here too much. I know where I belong."

"I suppose you're right. It's good that you have a solid sense of who you are and where you'll be happy. Not everyone has that. Be careful, don't let that cloud your feelings for Andi. You know you still care for her."

"Yeah. I do. When I saw her today, my first impulse was to throw my arms around her and hold her and never let her go. I wanted to kiss her so badly. I didn't. I barely held her hand in the car. I'm so afraid of letting her in again and having her blow me off."

"It's a whole new ballgame, now, buddy. She's not married now. She's free to be with you if you both want this."

"Right. I know. She's only been free for a short time. I'm not sure if she really wants me or if she simply feels safe with me."

"Then ask her. Tell her that's part of what's bothering you. You told me to take a risk with Carrie..."

"That was different. She didn't do anything to you except love you."

"And feed me. She did that, too." Kelly heard a little laugh from Shawn's end.

"True. I doubt if Andi would be doing much in the way of feeding me, other than lunch. She does do lunch nicely."

"See, there's that. You could do worse."

"I really don't see how your situation is like mine at all. Carrie liked you right away. Andi was an ice queen in the beginning. Carrie was the one that held you two together. Andi tore us apart."

"In your story, I'm thinking you're Carrie. Sort of. Well, maybe not so much. You carried Andi around with you like a weight for months after she left."

"I know, I had a hard time getting over her."

"You know you didn't actually get over her at all. You didn't even go out with anyone else all that time. That wasn't like you at all."

"No, I guess it wasn't..." She sat back down next to Piper.

"You mostly had your head down working, other than the times you were over here, from what I could see."

"Except I did have lunch with Elise a few times."

"Right. I bet that helped a lot, didn't it?"

"No, not really, I guess. I thought being around Elise by herself would help me stop thinking about Andi. I have to admit now that it didn't help at all."

"You still had that little connection to Andi through Elise. It kept that little spark of hope alive, I'm betting."

"I guess it did. Elise is a very nice woman and I enjoyed her company even without Andi."

"I've no doubt she's as sweet as you say. She likes you, so she must have good taste." Shawn laughed. "Aw...come on, you can laugh a little about this."

Kelly grinned, and then snickered. "All right. That was funny. I guess I'm trying to see this whole thing from a logical point of view. Just as I thought I was about to let go of my feelings for Andi, she shows up again with this story of hers and tells me she cares for me and has for months. I don't know how to deal with it."

"How would you like to deal with it?"

Kelly stood up again and resumed pacing. "My first impulse was to throw my arms around her, hold her close, tell her that somehow we'll work everything out, and it'll all be great."

"What's stopping you from doing exactly that?"

"What are you, now, a psychotherapist?"

"Nope, simply trying to help. I was no good to myself, that's for sure. I'm hoping I can help you the way you helped me. That's all. So, answer the question."

"I forgot the question."

"What's stopping you from throwing your arms around Andi, telling her you care about her, and working everything out from there?"

"Is that what I said? Well, I guess that's really what I want and I'm still scared."

"Of what? That she might leave again and not come back? Something tells me that's probably not going to happen. Her aunt lives here. She'll always come back."

"It's more...that she'll meet someone in New York that's more her type and fall for her and then there'd be the 'dear Kelly' thing."

"Here we go again. Listen, have you thought about the fact that something could happen like that to you? I mean, what if you met someone else who was more suited to you, who lived here and wanted to stay right here and had no other ambitions? Then what?"

"If I was with Andi, I wouldn't be looking even if someone else fell into my lap."

"Okay, then, what makes you think Andi would feel any differently?"

"I don't know. I guess because...well...I..." Kelly groped for an answer. "I don't know."

"Look, it sounds like your first date went well. When are you going to be together again?"

"I told her I'd make dinner at my house tomorrow night. Oh, and you two are invited. I wanted to keep this casual, not a romantic supper. Tell me you'll come."

"I need to square it with Carrie, of course. You can plan on us being there. About six, then?"

"Yeah, the usual. I'm going to grill some steaks."

"What can we bring?"

"Nothing. I've got it all covered. If you want, you could bring some ice cream. Carrie brought ice cream the time she came over while you were on your trip with AJ. Wait, I don't think that would be a good idea. I spilled chocolate sauce all over her at that one. Plus, that cookout didn't go very well for her and it might bring back some bad memories. Never mind. I'll think of something else. Just bring yourselves."

"Tell you what, we'll bring a bottle of wine to have with supper. Does that work?"

"That works. I want to entertain you guys for once."

"Are you sure you aren't showing off your culinary skills for a prospective partner?" Shawn laughed. "Hey, I'm all for that, by the way."

"Very funny. Just show up at six, okay?"

.

Chapter Twenty-seven

KELLY HAD MARINATED THE steaks all afternoon. The potatoes were baked in foil wrappers, waiting to be heated again on the grill. The ears of corn, still in their green leaves, sat in the sink in water, ready to be put on the grill as well. She had opted for some strawberries with vanilla ice cream for dessert, figuring that couldn't cause as much of a problem as ice cream sauce could if dropped. A cooler with beer and soda on ice sat at the ready on the lanai, where they'd eat. All her bases were covered. Her company would arrive any minute. She was ready.

She picked up Piper and while she scratched Piper's ears she looked around at the house she had probably spent more time working on than any other she had renovated. She always tried not to get attached to any of them because it was her business to make them comfortable and homey, sell them, and move on to the next house. Somehow, though, she knew it was going to be hard to let go of this one and it was getting close to time to do exactly that. She snuggled Piper to her and realized that this was the only home Piper had known with her.

She had her eye on the next one she was interested in taking on. It was in the style of the old cracker houses, except this one was built in the last thirty years or so. She thought the owners might let it go for a good price. Before she did that, she was going to have to sell the current project. It wouldn't take long. She knew it would sell quickly. All her renovations did. For some reason, she found herself wishing she didn't have to sell this one.

She didn't have long to ponder her next move as she heard a car in front of her house and so did Piper. Somehow, she knew Shawn and Carrie would arrive first. A look out the front window confirmed just that, with Andi arriving immediately after them.

As Kelly opened the door, Piper ran out barking her greeting to their guests. Carrie had scarcely released Andi from a hug as Piper reached her and she quickly picked up the wiggly little dog. Andi started to take Shawn's offered hand, however she reached to hug her as well. After an appropriate amount of dog kisses on Carrie's face, Piper resumed barking her hellos as Carrie held her and Andi and Shawn both scratched her ears. Kelly watched all of them acting like old friends. Andi appeared to eat it all up like one of Carrie's pies and Piper looked like she was in dog heaven. They seemingly hadn't even noticed her yet.

"I'm so glad to see you again," Carrie said to Andi.

"I'm very happy to be back. I had a wonderful time the last time I saw you two. Shawn, your book now occupies a much-honored spot on my bookshelf. I treasure that autographed copy you gave me."

"It was my pleasure to give it to you." Shawn grinned. "And here comes our human host."

The other two saw Kelly at the same time. Andi was closest and at first stood back, apparently unsure of what to do. Carrie and Shawn both hugged Kelly, and finally, Andi came for her hug. Kelly felt her arms close around Andi and Andi's body seemed to melt into hers briefly. If they hadn't been in Kelly's driveway, Kelly knew she'd have kissed her right there on the spot. To anyone else, it looked like a couple of old friends in a brief embrace.

Shortly, they all settled into the lanai and everyone engaged in small talk before Kelly retrieved the steaks from the kitchen to put on the outside grill. In no time, the tantalizing aroma of grilling steak made its way into the lanai every time Kelly opened the door to check on them. The baked potatoes and corn went onto the grill and in seemingly no time dinner was ready.

"So, you can cook, too," Andi said to Kelly in between bites of steak. "This is amazing."

"Yeah, she can cook. Well, she can grill, anyway." Carrie was chuckling. "I don't know why I always think she needs to be fed by someone else."

"I don't, either," Kelly said. "But I like being invited to supper. I suppose I could grill a roast, but that might not be pretty. Besides, you're a much better cook than I am."

"Ah, compliments will get you invited back for more meals, that's for sure," Carrie said. "You did a great job on this one."

"Why, thank you. That's high praise, coming from you."

"I agree, you did a great job, Kelly." Andi picked up her corn. "Thanks for inviting me."

"Aw...you guys want me to cook for you again. I can see what you're up to." Kelly laughed. "Well, I'd be happy to, just as long as you don't mind having whatever you eat come off my grill."

"I'll have to admit it's fun being cooked for," Carrie said. "I do love being the chef. On the other hand, being on the receiving end is great sometimes, too. And no," she looked pointedly at Kelly, "this isn't a hint to invite us over more often. You know I like feeding you. So, Andi, what've you been up to? It's been a long time since we've seen you."

"Well, I don't know how much Kelly told you, so I'm going to jump right in. I went back to New York because I was getting a divorce."

"We were surprised to hear that, for sure," Carrie said.

"I hope you didn't mind that I told them," Kelly said.

"No, I don't. It's all over now and to tell you the truth, I'm finding that I love being here in Florida." She looked over at Kelly. "I'm thinking about buying a place here, in fact."

"Really?" Carrie glanced at Kelly before returning to Andi. "When did you decide that?"

"Actually, I thought about it last fall. I sort of knew things were done between me and my ex by the time I came down here. I didn't realize how done they were until she asked me for a divorce. I knew at that moment it was completely over and I could stop fooling myself. I couldn't make any real plans until things were final. Once they were, I knew the next thing I wanted was to be here."

"Couldn't have anything to do with our Kelly, now could it?" Carrie asked, smiling.

"You could say that. You could say it has a lot to do with Kelly." She looked back over at Kelly. "Aunt Elise has loved coming down here for ages and I guess I've also gotten the bug from her. Since she's going to be living here full-time soon, I want a place to come to that's my own. I don't want to stay with her all the time, as pleasant as that is. So, I'm planning to engage an agent to find me the perfect home here."

"Wow. That sounds great. I hope we'll be seeing more of you, then," Shawn said.

"I sure hope so. I'd like to think that you might be happy to come to my house to visit sometimes."

Kelly hadn't said much of anything so far in the conversation. At first, she'd been speechless, preferring to listen and watch. Now she decided to chime in. "I'm sure we'd all be happy to come visit you whenever you're here. I'm assuming you'd use it like a vacation home?"

"Actually, I'm thinking of making it my home."

"But what about your gallery and all that?" Carrie said. "How can you run it from here?"

Andi laughed. "You've heard of the internet, right? Plus, I have a couple of great people on my staff there. They took care of things while

I was down here taking R and R with Aunt Elise last fall. I'm thinking of branching out and finding another place in Fort Myers or Naples for another gallery. I'm doing the research now."

"Again wow. I'm surprised," Kelly said. "I had no idea you were that serious."

Andi smiled at Kelly. "Now you know how serious I am. I love it here. Plus, I'd love to be closer to my aunt after she moves down here. I'm not saying I won't be going back to New York on a regular basis for business. I've already discussed this with Aunt Elise and she's fine with me using her place while I'm there so I don't have to maintain two homes. She plans to keep her place there because it's perfect for Christmas entertaining and she still loves to be in the city for the holidays or to visit friends off and on. Who knows, though, she might decide to spend part of the holidays here if I'm here."

"Well, well. Looks like we'll be seeing more of you soon. I'm looking forward to that, for sure." Carrie patted Andi's arm.

"Me, too," Shawn said.

Everyone looked at Kelly, who was still looking a bit dazed. "Me three. I hope you find what you're looking for here."

"I do, too," Andi said, looking into Kelly's eyes. "I have high hopes."

Chapter Twenty-eight

DINNER WAS OVER AND the bottle of wine emptied.

"We need to head home." Shawn patted Carrie's arm. She stretched as she and Carrie stood up. "Carrie has to be at work early tomorrow morning."

Carrie nodded. "Yeah, I promised Rich I'd call one of our German clients in the morning, their time. That makes it very early our time with that six hour time difference." Carrie hugged Andi as they were leaving. "I hope we'll be seeing much more of you now. I want you to know you're welcome at our home any time, with or without Kelly." She handed Andi a business card. "The office info is on the front, and here's my phone number on the back if you need anything. Anything at all."

"Thank you," Andi said. "I hope to see lots more of you guys, too. By the way, Shawn, I've made some of my friends jealous now that I've met one of their favorite authors."

Shawn grinned. "Thanks for the compliment. I'm glad they enjoy my work."

Shawn and Carrie both hugged Kelly, then they were gone, leaving Kelly and Andi waving to them at the door. Kelly was struck with how natural that felt. The evening had the same feel as that dinner at Shawn and Carrie's months ago, with everyone relaxed and chatting away about whatever. It'd felt like those months had melted away.

"You could stay for some coffee if you'd like," Kelly said as she shut the door.

"I'd like," Andi replied, putting her hand on Kelly's cheek. "But first, there's something else I'd like."

Andi's lips were soft, yielding, and oh yes, as wonderful as that night on the beach. Kelly felt her arms move around Andi, pulling her close as the kiss deepened and their bodies melted into each other. Kelly ended the kiss, keeping her arms around Andi.

"I..." Kelly started. "Wow. That was nice."

"It was. I've been wanting to do that since I got here."

"I've been wanting to do that practically since I first saw you. Well, not right away, but soon after we met. You are one luscious woman, Andi. I just never seem to know what to make of you."

"Ah, I'm a mystery woman. Interesting. I don't think I've been that before. I always thought of myself as boring."

"You? Boring? Not a chance."

Kelly took a deep breath as she released Andi and reached for her hand. "I do think we need to take this slow. You make me nervous."

"I think I like this." Andi grinned. "I make you nervous? Why?"

"I'm not quite sure. Let me put the coffee on and let's sit in the kitchen."

A few minutes later, coffee mugs full, they were sitting at the kitchen nook table. "I need to say some things to you." Kelly put her mug down and reached for Andi's hand. "I've been thinking. I do want to see if this will work between us, somehow. I have a question for you first."

"Fire away."

"I know I want to be with you. No doubts. Yes, you do make me feel safe. You also make me feel wonderful. You make me feel warm all over. You make me smile. You make me feel things I haven't felt in a long time. So yes, I'm very sure."

"I had to ask. Look, I know it won't be easy for either of us. If you're really planning to spend more time here, maybe it will work."

Andi reached with her other hand to cover Kelly's. "I'm making the plans now. I want you, Kelly. I care very much for you and I'm trying so hard to prove to you that I do."

"I can see that. I guess Shawn and Carrie could see it. They never leave that quickly after supper. I'm sure they figured we needed some time alone." She smiled. "Maybe we do. Need some time alone, I mean. I'd always tried to avoid being alone with you for very long. I never wanted you to think that I was pushing you for anything more than friendship. Despite all that, I started caring for you more than I should have. I had no idea you felt the same way."

"What about that wonderful kiss on the beach?"

Kelly shook her head slowly. "I shouldn't have done that."

"Why not?"

"Afterward, I felt like I was out of line. It was an impulse. I looked at you, and…"

"And what? Didn't I look like I wanted you to kiss me?"

"Well, yes, you did…"

"I really did want you to kiss me."

"I felt bad afterward, though. Like I shouldn't have."

"Kelly, I dreamed about that kiss for months. I held onto that kiss. I relived that kiss over and over and I'm so glad it happened. It felt wonderful. It felt right. I wanted more, but I didn't have the right to involve you in my problems back then. That's why I had to leave. Believe me I never stopped thinking about that kiss."

"I had no idea. I thought I'd overstepped and was mistaken about what you were trying to tell me. I thought you left because I chased you away or because I was solely someone to have fun with and playtime was over. I even imagined that you might have gone back to Jo."

"Oh, my God, no!" Andi held her hands up in a stop motion. "That was never going to happen."

"Well, I went over so many scenarios in my head, so many reasons why you might've left like that. I had no information to base anything on other than you left the morning after I kissed you."

Andi hung her head, sighed heavily, and then looked back into Kelly's eyes. "I'm so sorry. I don't know how I can ever make that up to you. At least now you know what happened even though I was totally in the wrong for leaving like I did."

"Well, yes you were..." Kelly put her elbow on the table, her chin in her hand, eyes locked on Andi's.

"And I was totally wrong for not telling you anything and not answering the phone or returning your texts."

"Yes, you were."

"And I so want to put that all behind us. I know you said you forgave me, so now I'd love to see where this leads for us. Can we do that? We could stay in and watch television or watch a movie together or go dancing somewhere if you'd like to do that. I have very simple wants and mostly I want to spend time with you."

"I enjoyed lunch yesterday even though I was a bit nervous. It was fun, I have to admit. You even drank that grog stuff." Kelly grinned, picking up her coffee mug and took a sip.

"Yes, I did. It wasn't that bad." Andi laughed, then she took a swig from her mug as if she was drinking the grog again. "Oh, by the way, you do make good coffee."

"Thanks. I've never gotten around to showing you the rest of the house, have I? Would you like to see it now that it's finished?"

"I'd love to. I noticed the last time I was here that the bannister was installed. It's beautiful. Lots of hands will enjoy touching it on their way up and down."

"Thanks, I worked hard on it. Since you can see it from the front door, I thought of it more as a design element than simply something to hold onto for safety. I'm glad you appreciate it. Bring your coffee and I'll give you the fifty-cent tour. You've already seen the kitchen and living room, now I'll show you the little extras I put in to make them special."

Kelly opened the lower kitchen cabinets and demonstrated the slide-out drawers inside the doors. There were two large drawers under the cooktop for pots and pans and the like.

"How did you come up with the drawers? That's a wonderful idea."

"I got tired of trying to reach back into the cabinets for stuff. Open either of those two cabinet doors." She pointed to the upper cabinets near the stove.

Andi opened one of the indicated cabinet doors. "Wow, built-in spice racks. Nice touch"

"Beats having them all jumbled up in the cabinet or taking up space on the countertop. This isn't a very large house and keeping things tidy will make it look a bit bigger."

"Very true. More surprises upstairs?"

Kelly just grinned. "You'll see. Come on. I think you'll like it." She led the way upstairs, with Piper at first trotting along behind then running ahead and disappearing at the landing.

Andi climbed the stairs, running her hand along the bannister. "Wow, I might have to hire you to make my new house as great as this one."

"Oh, you haven't seen anything yet."

"Okay, now I'm looking forward to..." her mouth dropped open as she reached the top of the stairs and Kelly stepped aside. "What a wonderful spot!"

The stair landing led into a small sitting area with bookshelves on two sides and a round, paned, stained glass window looking out into the back yard. The stained glass design was simple a lighthouse on a sandy beach. Kelly had placed an overstuffed chair and a small round table with a lamp and room for a cup or glass on it right in front of the window. The seated person could look out the window or down the stairs to the front door. Piper had jumped into a little dog bed next to the chair. A small hassock sat at the ready on the other side of the table.

"What was this space before you transformed it? It's very cozy."

"Oh, it was a storage area, believe it or not. Semi-useless unless someone wanted to plumb it and put in a washer and dryer. Now it serves a purpose. I've sat up here a lot since I did this. Piper and I like to read up here. Well, I read and Piper snoozes." Kelly laughed. "She doesn't mind if I read out loud to her, though."

"I bet she doesn't. It's probably a soothing sound. I was just thinking that if this is an example of what you do to all the houses you renovate, I'm sure you have no problem selling them as soon as they're done."

"Not usually. I use the same realtor each time and she knows what kind of work I do and how to point out each house's unique details to prospective buyers. On the last one, there was a bidding war and I got more for it than I hoped. That sure was nice. Want to see the rest now?"

"I'm ready. I'm sure there are more surprises in store."

"You're right, there are." Kelly opened the door to the left off the hall revealing a small bedroom. A flick of the light switch lit up a lamp on the chest of drawers. "I always think of this as the guest room because it's so tiny. The way the house is laid out, I couldn't enlarge it without moving the staircase or the like. That would've been way too much trouble and energy. Instead, I made it into a little garret room that a guest or two would find fun to stay in for a short while."

"It is quite small." Andi stood in the doorway. "What was this area before you remodeled?"

"It appeared to be more of an attic than a room at the time I bought the house. It's over the carport. I only had room to put in a pocket-sized closet, so I doubt someone would want to live in here long-term."

While Kelly stood in the doorway, Andi walked in to find a double bed with wicker headboard, white painted bead board on the walls and light blue ceiling. The bed, which took up most of the room, had a pale blue chenille spread on it which appeared to be a shade slightly darker than the ceiling. Tiny wicker night stands topped with glass, one on each side of the bed, and the small chest of drawers were the only other items in the room.

"I love this. It's perfect for company. You might have a hard time getting them to leave, in fact. How did you come up with painting the ceiling blue?"

"I don't know, it simply came to me. The room was rather dark. I didn't want everything white in here and I thought it might look like the sky."

Andi walked around the room, running her hand along the plush chenille bedspread. She stopped at the chest of drawers, touching it in an almost caressing gesture. "You made this, didn't you?" she asked in a near whisper.

"I did. How did you guess?" Kelly leaned against the door jamb and took another sip of her coffee.

"It feels like you made it. It seems to have some of your spirit in it."

"You're not going all metaphysical on me, now, are you?"

"No, the way the wood feels gave you away. Your pieces have a very...well...smooth feeling, for lack of a better word. They're very tactile. They don't just look good, they beg to be touched. Whoever ends up with this house might want to keep that chest."

"I'll probably offer the house with or without the furniture. I've sold some of these houses to snowbirds and they like buying places with nearly everything there, ready to move in...turnkey, if you will." Kelly motioned toward the door.

"I love what I've seen so far. Lead on." Andi raised her mug in salute, then drained the last of her coffee. Kelly took the mug from her and placed their two mugs on the small hall table.

Piper had been watching them from her hallway vantage point. Now she got up and followed them across the hall, then trotted ahead into a much larger room which was obviously the master bedroom. As soon as Kelly flicked the lights on, Piper made a well-practiced leap onto the bed and laid there with her face on her paws, watching them.

"This used to be two smaller bedrooms," Kelly explained. "I combined them and made a bathroom out of part of one of them. You may have noticed the other door in the hall—the bathroom opens to the hallway as well. There wasn't room to put in two bathrooms up here, so if a guest is staying across the hall, they have to share the one and only on this floor. There's a compact bathroom with a shower downstairs and a small room with a twin bed connected to it. A single guest could stay there and have their own bath. Or a new owner could use it as a small office. I slept in there for quite a while during the upstairs renovations and it was fine. This, however, is much nicer to live in."

This room also had the white bead board on the walls as wainscoting, giving it a bright, airy feel. Kelly had painted a very pale coral pink above the wainscoting and on the ceiling. Instead of a bedspread, a quilt with various coral, green, and blue tropical prints in it covered the antique-looking iron bed. The decorations were spare, obviously well thought out. A comfortable chair and small table sat under the window at one end of the room.

"I love this room, too," Andi said. "You definitely have an eye for decorating as well as building things. It's very relaxing and it's warm and welcoming, too."

Kelly smiled, watching as Andi walked slowly around the room—first looking out the window then running her hand along the footboard of the bed. She stopped at the dresser.

"You didn't make this one. I can tell it's not from a store. Is it something precious to you?" Andi asked.

"You do have good instincts. My grandfather made it for me before he died. That goes where I go, obviously. Whoever buys this place will have to get their own dresser for this room."

"Of course." She reached for a drawer pull, looking at Kelly for permission to open it. After Kelly nodded her approval, she pulled the drawer open a few inches to look at its construction. "It's beautifully made. This piece could stand as a work of art as well." She shook her head and pushed the drawer closed. "I can sure see where you get your talent."

Grinning, Kelly walked over to the dresser and pulled one of the drawers all the way out. She lifted it above Andi's head and told her to look at the bottom of it. There on the underside of the drawer was burned a message.

Andi read it out loud, "'For Kelly with love from Grandpop Bradley June 1997.' Was that a special occasion?"

"The year I turned twenty-two. I had recently graduated from college and I guess he figured I needed some real furniture. I've moved it with me ever since." She slid the drawer smoothly back into the dresser. "What do you think? Is this livable for a young couple or an older couple that can still climb stairs?"

"Anyone would be happy here unless they had a big family. This whole house is perfect. I love everything in it." Andi moved closer and put her arms around Kelly, her head on Kelly's shoulder as Kelly's arms went around her. "You're amazing," she said into Kelly's shoulder

Kelly felt her heart pounding. She had wondered what it'd be like to see Andi here in her bedroom. To kiss her here. Andi felt so good in her arms. She felt so right. Taking it slowly sounded so...slow...now.

Andi's face looked up at her with that same expectant look, however once again Andi didn't wait for Kelly to kiss her. Kelly felt Andi's lips on hers and she felt herself melting. Their kiss deepened, mouths open, tongues playing, and their bodies welded together. Kelly thought her legs could collapse under her, taking them both to the floor. She ended the kiss abruptly.

"I...I didn't bring you up here to..." she began.

"Maybe you didn't, maybe you did. It doesn't matter," Andi whispered. "Kelly, I...I want you. I look in your eyes and I know you're the one. Every time I find out something new about you, I care for you even more. Are you telling me you don't want me?"

"Oh, God, no." Kelly brushed Andi's hair at her temples lightly with her fingers. "I want you, I just..."

"What? Do you still doubt me?"

"No. I don't."

"Then what?"

When Kelly didn't say anything more, Andi reached up to put her hand over Kelly's hand in her hair. She brought both their hands to her lips, kissed Kelly's palm, and placed it on her breast, over her heart. "Can you feel my heart beating? It's been yours for a while now. Yours and only yours. And I want you to claim it."

At the touch of her hand to Andi's breast, Kelly swallowed hard. She knew she was in deep.

Chapter Twenty-nine

KELLY'S HAND HADN'T MOVED from where Andi placed it over her heart, and she had pulled just inches away and gazed into Andi's eyes. "Andi, you know I care about you."

"I know that." Andi smiled. She placed a brief kiss on Kelly's lips.

"And you can tell I want you."

"I can tell. Is there a 'but' somewhere in there?" Another little kiss.

"I thought so, now I think I lost it." Kelly grinned as she wrapped her arms around Andi and pulled her closer. She closed her eyes and felt Andi melting into in her arms. She had dreamt of doing this so many times. She could smell Andi's hair, her shampoo something sweet and fresh. Her fragrance was also a clean, soap and water.

After what seemed like forever she opened her eyes and looked into Andi's. "I so want to believe all of this is real."

"It is. We're here. Together. Alone."

"In my bedroom."

Andi grinned. "Yes, in your bedroom. What should we do next?"

"Hmm...I don't know. What do you want to do?" Kelly grinned back.

"Well, it's your house..."

"And you're the guest, so..."

Andi's lips on Kelly's stopped the conversation and answered the question. Andi's hands on Kelly's face, then the back of her head, pulling her into the kiss, their mouths admitting each other's tongues to probe, taste, and play.

Whatever Kelly's brain might have been trying to say, her body and heart shut it down. Her heart was ready for this. Her body wanted Andi. Now. If Andi left tomorrow and never returned, she'd still have tonight. She wanted Andi now and she knew Andi wanted her. She could feel it down to her core. She felt herself open the gate in the last fence between them and Andi walked in.

Kelly's fingers found the bottom of Andi's T-shirt. She reached beneath it and touched the soft skin on Andi's back. She could hear herself breathing heavier as a soft moan escaped from Andi's lips. She reached down and caressed her behind, pulling her closer. Andi's fingers were reaching for Kelly's shirt, pulling it up, forcing them back apart as her shirt came off over her arms.

Andi's T-shirt came off next, exposing a black lace push-up bra. Kelly kissed the soft exposed part of Andi's breast and heard her moan in response. She reached to unclasp the front closure on Andi's bra, releasing the rest of her and dropping the bra to the floor.

"You're so beautiful," Kelly whispered into Andi's ear. "I do want you. I want you so much it hurts."

"I've waited so long to hear you say that," Andi whispered back. "I want you, too. Now." Andi's lips were on Kelly's again, hard. The kisses deeper and more demanding as she reached for Kelly's sports bra and pulled that off over her head, then quickly unbuttoned her shorts and slid them down where Kelly stepped out of them and kicked them away.

Piper must've figured out that she should move somewhere else, because she jumped off the bed and into another little dog bed near the dresser, where she promptly laid down and ignored them.

Kelly reached to throw back the quilt before she picked Andi up and placed her gently on the bed. As she lay down next to her, she stopped and looked at her for a few seconds. "You really are beautiful. You take my breath away."

Tears escaped from Andi's eyes as she tried to keep from crying. "I've never been with anyone who said anything remotely that sweet to me. Ever."

Kelly gently wiped the tear from each of her eyes with her thumb, then kissed her eyelids. "Then you're overdue. They were blind," she whispered into Andi's ear.

"I…I so want you. You have no idea." Andi pulled Kelly to her for a kiss.

Kelly whispered back, "I want you, too." She traced the outline of Andi's face with a finger while gazing into her eyes, and then traced a line of kisses from Andi's ear down her throat to the swell of her breasts as Andi moaned her name and made little whimpering noises. She cupped one breast, feeling its softness in her hand as her tongue played around Andi's now hardened nipple and sucked on it. She heard her breathe in sharply in pleasure as she kissed and licked her way to Andi's other breast.

Kissing her way down Andi's tummy, she slid off Andi's shorts and black lace bikinis and tossed them to the floor. Her hand slowly explored the silken skin on the inside of Andi's thigh as her lips returned to Andi's. Their tongues danced as the kiss deepened. Her fingers explored Andi's wet center—her erect clit and the warm wetness below, knowing her own was just as wet.

Andi pushed against Kelly's hand as she stroked her, matching her rhythm, their breathing ragged from desire. "Oh, yes, oh, yes," over and over as her hips ground harder against Kelly's hand, bringing Kelly's own desire closer and closer to the top.

Andi cried out Kelly's name in release as Kelly came seconds later in response. Both breathing hard, they laid wrapped in each other's arms and legs for a few minutes, unable to move.

"Oh. My. God." Andi took a deep breath and hugged Kelly closer. "That was amazing. You're amazing."

"So are you." Kelly rolled over on her back, pulling Andi with her, wrapped in her arms. Andi lay dozing and Kelly no longer had any doubts that Andi was the one she wanted. She knew they'd work out the whole "not living here" thing somehow. They had to. She moved a small strand of hair out of Andi's face and knew her heart had found a home. They only had to figure it all out.

Chapter Thirty

"I'M GUESSING THAT you and Kelly made up, since you didn't come back last night?" Elise smiled and patted Andi's hand as they sat across from each other in the kitchen nook.

"Yes, you could say that. I think I'm definitely forgiven."

"You have quite a glow about you." Andi blushed as Elise grinned at her. "I'm glad. You know, I wish you two had met before you got involved with Jo, although I can't imagine how that would've happened."

"I know. It was serendipity that we met at all. If you hadn't wanted those bookcases and if the construction company hadn't sent her...well, we might never have run into each other. So, I guess I should thank you for setting all of this in motion."

"For what it's worth, you're welcome. I'm happy to see you happy. So now what? What's next?"

Andi took a deep breath. "Well, what's next is that we need to have some time to be together and see how it goes. I still have a business to run, however I think we will work it all out. Your idea of another gallery here in Fort Myers or Naples could be exactly the thing. Do you know any good real estate agents who handle commercial property?"

"I'm sure I can find someone for you if you'd like me to get the ball rolling. Friends of friends, if you know what I mean. Everyone around here seems to have some connection. I'll ask around if you'd like."

"That'd be great, thanks. Oh, and one more thing. Last night Kelly told me she's just about finished with the house she's currently renovating. She said she'll put it on the market soon and when she does, I want it."

"Really? That nice, huh?"

"Wait till you see it. You've seen what she can do with a bookcase, try to imagine that on a whole house."

"Well, you did say you wanted a place here. If that's what you want..."

"Aunt Elise, it's wonderful. It's cozy. Exactly enough room. I'm sure I want it."

"Okay, then. Why don't you simply tell Kelly you want it and pay her what she asks?"

"I could. I know she needs to sell it to move on to the next renovation and I can offer her a cash deal. What's worrying me is that since I want to live there with her, it might feel like I was pushing our relationship forward quickly when we just got together. That might be moving too fast for her. Is there some way I can buy it without her knowing it's me?"

"I don't know. We'll have to look into it. Are you sure you want that house and not a condo?"

"I'm sure. I've never been so sure of anything like this before. It feels completely right."

"Okay, let's see what we can do. I'll ask around about an agent, and we'll go from there. It would be nice to find one that handles both residential and commercial property. I have an attorney here in town, too. If we need to, I can check with her and see what she says about buying property."

"Thank you. You're always there every time I need help and I do appreciate it."

"I love you, sweetie. And I love being able to help you any way I can. I have a thought. Does Kelly know the name of your gallery or the name you hold it under?"

"No, she doesn't. Why? Are you thinking what I'm thinking?"

"If it's to buy it as your company, yes, that's what I'm thinking. You're incorporated, right?"

"Right. I guess I could buy it under the company name, which isn't the same as the SoHo gallery anyway. After it's all done, I could sign it over to myself as personal property. That might work, as long as it's all legal."

"We can run it by my attorney and see what she says. She's used to getting oddball questions from her clients, I'm sure."

"I bet she is." Andi laughed. "Sounds good. If we need to, we could call her this afternoon if she's available."

"I'll call around about a realtor first and set up an appointment, then see if my attorney will be in her office if we need to call her while the realtor is here. I love doing this. I'm getting excited for you!"

"Aunt Elise, you're wonderful. You always seem to have a solution to every problem I come up with. How do you do it?"

"Sweetie, I've been around the block a few times. There's not much I haven't had to deal with myself already. Now, I'll admit I haven't tried to buy property from someone I was interested in as a lover."

"No, I'm sure you haven't. That didn't stop your brain from coming up with some great ideas for solutions."

"Ah, well, what can I say? When you've got it, you've got it." Elise grinned again, holding her hands up.

"And you've definitely got it. You've always had it. I still say it's amazing you've stayed single for so long. I'm surprised someone hasn't snatched you up."

"You have to make yourself available for something like that to happen. I really haven't been interested in anyone else since…" Her voice trailed off, then she waved her hand as if she dismissed the thought. "Anyway, I've been quite busy."

"One of these days, you need to not be so busy. When will you have time for you?"

Elise took a deep breath. "I have time for me. I don't know if I have time for someone else in my life. Perhaps I'll be able to make time if the right one falls into my lap." She winked at Andi. "Kind of like Kelly did for you."

"Right…well, here's to hoping that someone wonderful magically appears into your life, too." Andi held up her glass of soda in salute.

Elise held hers up as well, then clinked her glass to Andi's as she smiled. "Sure. I'm not holding my breath."

Chapter Thirty-one

SOMETIMES THINGS JUST HAPPEN. Sometimes they happen for a reason, sometimes they don't. These words kept going through Kelly's mind as she mulled over the night before. Holding Andi in her arms, kissing her, touching her, making love with her, they all came when she wasn't sure she was ready for them. She knew she cared for Andi. Was she ready for a relationship with her?

Piper looked up at her as they enjoyed a Saturday morning on their lanai. Scratching Piper's ears absently, Kelly knew it wouldn't be long until this house would no longer be hers. It would sell quickly and she'd move on to the next house to renovate. It had always been fun before, exciting even. For some reason, today she was feeling rather melancholy about leaving this house.

Maybe it was because this was where she was living when she met Andi. This was where she was living when she adopted her adorable Piper. It was also where she was living when she watched Shawn and Carrie marry. She'd stayed in this house much longer than the other renovations, so that was probably it. It was only someplace she'd lived in longer. That's all.

No, that wasn't all. For some reason, this house had gotten to her. She'd spent more time working on it because it wanted her to. It needed her to. The house had given her a home. She had given it love back. And now she had to put it up for sale and move on. She wasn't going to be happy about it, but that's the way it was. She hoped whoever bought it would love it like she had.

Her real estate agent was on the way over to do the paperwork. Lauren Prescott had worked with her for several years and several houses. She always did a great job and the houses practically sold themselves the way Lauren presented them. She always knew exactly what to point out to each potential buyer and was great at getting the buyer to pay well for what they were getting. There had even been bidding wars on some of those houses. They were a great team. So why didn't she feel great this time?

Piper leaped off the loveseat and dashed for the door, barking. Must be Lauren. Piper could always hear someone pull into the driveway before Kelly knew they were there. She sometimes affectionately referred to Piper as her personal dog bell.

"Got another one for me?" Lauren asked as Kelly held the door for her. Lauren was old enough to be Kelly's mom, except she was not at all mom-like. She was taller than Kelly by several inches, trim and athletic-looking, with rather striking grey eyes and very light strawberry blonde hair. Kelly always thought she colored it because she didn't see any grey in it. If she did, it was a great job.

"It's been a while, hasn't it? Well, I've been working on this one for much longer than any of the others. I think you'll like it and I hope someone nice will want to buy it."

"You always say that...like the buyer is adopting the house." Lauren stopped still inside the door. "Wow, I love this. I can see you've done some amazing work in here, from standing in the entry. That stair bannister, for one, is gorgeous. It sure looks different than it did at the time you bought it."

"Well, that's the idea." Kelly closed the door behind them. "Come on back to the kitchen and let's chat first. Afterward, I'll give you the big tour."

Lauren's eyes moved constantly as they walked, taking in the cozy little living room. Kelly knew Lauren was going ka-ching every time she noticed a little detail that Kelly had put into this house that was unique. She wouldn't talk about an asking price until she had seen the whole thing in detail.

Kelly handed Lauren a bottle of Diet Coke, Lauren's staple drink. Lauren took a sip from the bottle after they sat at the kitchen nook table. "Wow, look at this tabletop. It's amazing. It's such a nice place to sit now and it'll be a big selling point. The little wooden table someone had pieced together and shoved into this spot before did it no justice. This thing even feels sweet to the touch."

"Thanks. I know you love built-ins, and this one was fun to make. I may do something like it again in another house."

"Now that would be nice. By the way, since you're getting ready to sell this one, I know you're looking for another one. If you have something in mind, tell me. I do have a few pictures here to show you. We can see if anything strikes a chord with you. If you see something you want to look at, all you have to do is say so and we can go look any time you want."

"Well, I've seen something I might be interested in at the right price. It's a cracker house..."

Lauren put up a hand to interrupt her, pulled a picture out of her folder, and slid it over for Kelly to see. "By any chance, could it be this one?" It was the one Kelly had driven by multiple times.

"That's the one. Wow, do you know me or what? Do you have more pictures? Is it a mess inside or is it worth saving?"

"I haven't seen the inside other than a few pictures posted on the MLS. I printed those out for you, as well. You can see them better than on a tiny laptop picture." She slid those pictures across the table as well.

It was fairly clear the house was not in pristine shape. It'd been well-used and probably somewhat abused over the decades, however that didn't rule it out as a possibility. "How big is the lot?" Kelly asked.

"Good sized. Probably as big as this one. I think it has potential as a fixer. Do you want to see the pictures of the other properties I picked out for you to see or do you already have your heart set on this one?"

"Let's look at the other pictures. While I still like that one, I'm not closed minded about other possibilities."

Lauren pulled out pictures of five other properties in various stages of handyman special condition. "There were more properties that fell into your usual category. These, including the one you already liked, seemed to be the best value as far as I could see. I've toured all the rest of them except for that cracker house."

Lauren sat quietly, taking sips from her Diet Coke. One of the things Kelly liked best about Lauren was that she knew when to shut up and let her look or think. She didn't get fidgety or try to break the silence with chatter. She simply sat there, sipped on her Diet Coke, and waited.

Kelly looked at the pictures of the other properties and decided she should at least look at a couple of the other ones. With the money she'd make off this one, she could probably afford to buy two more. That might be kind of silly since she could only work on one at a time and the other one would sit until she could get to it. Or would it? She could rent one of them out for a year or so until she was ready. It was worth considering, anyway.

Kelly finally made two piles of the pictures. "I've decided to look at these two plus the cracker house," she said, pushing the pile of the ones she wanted to see toward Lauren. She turned the other pictures upside down. "I'm not interested in seeing these. They don't speak to me at all."

Lauren picked up the pile Kelly wanted to see and put a paper clip on them. "Okay, I'll set up a time to tour these houses. I don't think anyone's living in any of them, so we can go any time you're ready. First things first, what about this one? Are you completely done with it, or nearly done?"

"I can't think of anything else that needs to be done for now. I suppose there are always things that I could do. You know how I get sometimes. I love how this one turned out. I almost wish I didn't have to sell it."

"I know. It's almost like your baby. Seems to me you've worked on this one longer than the others. I'm sure we'll find it a good new owner who'll love it and take care of it. Just for the heck of it, have you even considered finally keeping one for yourself? I mean, seriously, you need to settle down sometime with your own home."

"Well, yes, I have. It's just me and Piper and I don't know...I haven't decided yet. Sometime, yes. It could be soon."

"Oh...does that mean you have someone special in your life, finally?"

"Well, maybe. I'm not sure how it's going to work out. She owns an art gallery in New York and is a big city girl. I don't know if she'd be happy living here permanently. It's all in the beginning stages and..."

"Look, if it's supposed to be, it'll work out. I'd love to see you happy with someone special. You've paid your dues."

"Yes, I guess I have. Several times over." Kelly laughed then shook her head. "What a trail of dues-paying I've had. I always seem to fall either for the ones that are totally wrong for me or someone that's perfect for someone else. Oh well, that's been my life so far. Maybe it's my turn now. We'll see."

"Hey, we all learn. Look at me. I'm on my own again. Sharon seemed to love me and the life I live here in Florida. For some reason nine months ago she decided she couldn't stay after all and went back to Denver."

"I'm so sorry. I thought she was going to be part of your happy ever after. You two seemed so perfect together."

"Yeah, I thought so, too. I confess I could see it coming before she finally told me. You know, I'm not looking for another Carole. Carole was one of a kind."

"Yes, she was. I felt so bad for you after she died. You did have...what...fifteen great years together?"

"Yes, we did." Lauren took a deep breath, letting it out in a sigh. "Well, I'm not making a big effort to find someone, either. If the right one falls into my lap...hey, I'm not going to look the other way. I don't think anyone wants to be alone for the rest of her life, although I'd rather be alone than with the wrong person again."

"I feel the same way. We'll see if this one works out. I care very much about her and even if it turns out we're destined to only be good friends, so be it."

"I wish you luck. So...let's get back to the business at hand. How soon do you want me to put this one out there?"

"You can list it today if you want." Kelly breathed a small sigh, then smiled. "I'm ready as I'll ever be."

"Great. And I'm ready for the tour. From what I can see so far, this one's going to be a fast seller, as usual."

Chapter Thirty-two

ELISE PUNCHED IN THE number for Prescott Realty. Several of her friends told her Lauren Prescott was the best at what she did, finding the perfect properties for clients. She decided to talk to Ms. Prescott and see how she felt. The receptionist who answered the phone cheerfully put her right through to Lauren.

"Lauren Prescott. How can I help you?" Elise liked the sound of her voice right away. A rather full, round, alto sound, upbeat and genuine.

"Hi, I'm Elise Wainright. I'm calling because several friends here in Palm Harbour Isles recommended you."

"Well, that was nice of them. What can I help you with?"

"My niece owns an art gallery in New York. She's planning to open another one in this area and needs space. She's also interested in a small house here in Fort Myers. Do you handle commercial as well as residential properties?"

"Yes, I do. I'd be happy to discuss it with her. Is she available this afternoon? I can meet her wherever she'd like."

"Yes, she is. She's here visiting me, and will be here this afternoon. We'd love to have you come talk to us. She's looking for gallery space in Fort Myers or Naples but she wants a house in Fort Myers."

"Great. I'm sure I can help her find something she'll like. How about three? Does that sound convenient for you both? I assume you'll be there as well."

"Perfect. Yes, we will. If you'll give me your cell number, I'll text you my address."

Lauren recited her cell number. "I'll watch for your text, then see you at three."

"We'll see you then." Elise hit end on the phone, the smile on her face revealing it was just the beginning. She knew this meant a new life for Andrea and she couldn't wait to have her near her again and happy. Mostly the happy part. It was so time for it to happen. She loved Kelly and if things worked out she was going to be very excited to have Kelly in the family. But first things first. Andi was out doing errands, so Elise called her to let her know the real estate agent was coming at three.

"Excellent." Elise could hear the grin in her voice. "I'm so excited to get started on this project. I want that house, and starting another gallery will be so much fun. It'll be a lot of work and a lot of fun as well."

"Yes, it will. Are you coming home for lunch?"

"I'll be there. Kelly said she had an appointment this morning, so we won't see each other till later today."

"Tell you what, I'll have lunch ready if you give me a time."

"Twelve-thirty? Will that work out? I only have a couple more places to go."

"Works for me. How about BLT's for lunch?"

"Sounds great. I'll see you then."

At twelve-thirty on the nose Andi walked in the front door and headed for the kitchen. She tossed her bag on the kitchen island and gave Elise a hug.

Elise headed toward the kitchen nook, where their lunch was waiting. "So how did today's foray into the local art galleries go? What did you find?"

Andi slid onto the other bench and picked up her napkin. "Well, there are already quite a few galleries here in town. Lots of nice ones with some great pieces. I need to come up with a different promotion idea than simply Florida art, since there are several that specialize in it. I'll work on it. I can't stay here much longer this trip, with one of my best-selling artists opening a major showing in a week. If there's time, I'd like to look around in Naples, too."

"The agent coming this afternoon might have some ideas as well. She'd know the best areas for something like that, I'm sure."

At three on the nose, the doorbell rang. Andi answered the door and found Lauren standing there, putting out her hand.

"Hi, I'm Lauren Prescott. Are you Elise's niece?"

"Yes, I am. Andrea Wainwright. Nice to meet you." She shook Lauren's hand, stood aside, and waved her in. "Come on back to the lanai. Aunt Elise is out there and we can talk business in comfort. What can I get you to drink?"

"Oh, I'm not picky. If you happen to have a Diet Coke, I'd love it."

"A Diet Coke it is then." She led Lauren to the lanai and introduced her to her aunt. She watched Elise smile at Lauren and welcome her, leaving the lanai to fetch Lauren's soda before she heard the rest of the conversation. As she reached into the refrigerator, she realized she had seen a look on her aunt's face that she hadn't seen in a very long time. *It looked like...no...it couldn't be.*

By the time Andi returned to the lanai, Elise and Lauren were chatting like old buddies. They both looked up when Andi came back with the Diet Coke for Lauren. Elise and Andi were still nursing the second round of iced teas left over from lunch.

"So, your aunt has been vetting me. I hope I passed the test. Does she do this to everyone?" Lauren laughed as she reached for the soda put before her.

"Why, yes. Yes, she does. She does it very nicely, don't you think?" Andi grinned at her aunt.

"Yes, she does." Lauren winked at Elise, producing an almost immediate flush of color on Elise's cheeks. Lauren returned her attention to Andi. "I understand that you're looking for two things, a small house here in Fort Myers and gallery space either here or in Naples. Do I have that right?"

"Yes," Andi said. "I have a gallery in SoHo now, and I'm looking to expand to a second gallery here. I'd prefer to find space in a nice area here, or if not, in Naples. The house, however, must be here in Fort Myers."

Lauren opened her laptop. "And the house. Do you prefer one or two stories? On the water or not. That kind of thing."

"I have a house in mind, if it's up for sale yet." Andi gave her the address of Kelly's house.

"That house just came on the market today. It has lots of custom features. Have you seen it already?" Lauren cocked her head slightly as she looked at her. She pulled up the listing, showing the various pictures that she'd taken.

"Actually, I know Kelly. I don't want to make a big deal out of buying that house, but I do want it. It's perfect. I'm willing to pay whatever she's asking for it."

"Well, that's nice. No dickering? You want to make a full price offer?"

"No dickering. I know she wouldn't be asking something outrageous for it."

"You do know that's not in a neighborhood like this one. It's a regular middle-class area. Are you sure you want it? I've got some others that you might like, too."

"I'm sure. You could plop that house down on a desert island and I'd still want it."

"Okay, then, we'll write up an offer. Full asking price, right?"

"Yep. Unless someone else has already bought it, I want it."

"Kelly's renovations always go fast. However, I think this might set a record." Lauren laughed, a low, throaty sound that reminded Andi of Lauren Bacall in an old movie. She glanced over at Elise. Nope, it wasn't wasted on her, either. Elise was a huge Lauren Bacall fan. *Oh, funny...Lauren sounds like Lauren.* She just made the connection.

"How much do you want for earnest money?" Andi asked. "I'm ready to write a check. Or I can have my bank wire the money to you."

"$5,000 is fine. And if you have your checkbook with you, I'll take a check. Save the wire fees for closing. Since I'm the listing agent for that house, I know there isn't any other offer on the table right now. Looks like this house is going to be yours."

Andi grinned. She got up and left to get her checkbook. Somehow, she knew her aunt and Lauren were not going to be talking about real estate—not for long anyway. She managed to dawdle in her room for a few more minutes after the checkbook was located before walking slowly back down the hall. She wasn't trying to eavesdrop, yet she couldn't help hearing her aunt's laughter counterpointed by Lauren's. *Well, well. Aunt Elise has found a new friend.*

When she walked back into the lanai, it warmed Andi's heart to see a look on her aunt's face that hadn't seen in a very long time. She positively glowed.

"Okay, let's do this," Andi said to Lauren as she sat down.

After another round of sodas and the offer written for Kelly's house, Andi wanted to see what kinds of gallery space were available in the area. Lauren was ready for this, as well, with her laptop tabbed to a list with pictures. They settled on several in Fort Myers and one in Naples to go look at the next day.

An hour later, Andi got up. "Looks like I'm good to go. Let me know if she accepts my offer. Please remember that no matter what it takes to get it, I want it. I'd rather she didn't know it was me until closing if possible. For now, we can keep this as a purchase from a company in New York. If she asks, tell her it's a very nice woman looking for a winter home and she loved the pictures online. How's that?"

"Sounds good to me. I'll try to convince her to not ask very many more questions until the closing."

"You're good." Andi couldn't help smiling. "Very good."

It was Lauren's turn to grin. "Well, I've had lots of experience. Plus, I know Kelly and she trusts me. She knows I won't sell it to someone who's going to go in and tear out all her hard work. Meantime..." Lauren turned to Elise, "Do you have dinner plans? I have a banquet I need to go to this evening and I'd love it if you'd come with me. I know this is short notice. What do you think?"

Elise smiled. "Well, I don't have plans and I don't mind dressing up. Not black tie, I assume?"

"Cocktail attire."

"I can do that. What time?"

"I'll pick you up at seven." Lauren turned to Andi and grinned. "I'd like you to know, my intentions toward your aunt are strictly honorable."

"I'm sure they are. Just bring her back before the carriage turns back into a pumpkin."

Lauren and Elise laughed. "I'm sure we will," Elise said.

"All right, Miss Andi. I'll present your offer to Kelly and see if she bites. She should. It's a full price offer with no financing involved. It's a great offer, in fact. I'll call you right after I talk to her and tell you what she says."

Andi shook Lauren's hand. She decided to let Elise walk Lauren to the door without her hanging about and couldn't help the grin on her face once Elise returned to the lanai.

"So, what do you think of Lauren?" Andi asked as Elise reclaimed her seat at the table.

Elise took a sip of her tea. "She seems very pleasant and quite knowledgeable. No wonder she comes so highly recommended."

"That's not what I meant, and you know it. What do you think of her personally?"

"I like her. She seems like a nice woman who's also funny and smart."

"So...you aren't going to this thing tonight because you want to help my deal along, right?"

"What? No. Of course not. I'd never do that. It sounded like a fun evening, that's all." Elise really did seem to twinkle.

"If you're sure. I wouldn't want you to put yourself through another one of those rubber chicken things on my account." Andi tried to look serious.

"I'm sure it won't be. In fact, I'm pretty sure I went to the same banquet last year and it was quite entertaining. I don't remember seeing her there, though, and I think I'd remember her. Those grey eyes are amazing."

"I bet you would have. She's quite striking. I didn't notice her eyes. I must've been paying more attention to the paperwork or the pictures." She giggled. "But she's more your type than mine, that's for sure."

"Now don't get carried away, young lady. It's only an evening out. Besides, your type is now Kelly. I'm so glad things are working out so far. I just know you two belong together."

"I think so, too. We'll make it all work. I know we will."

"Okay, now that we're done buying you a house, I need to go pick out an outfit for tonight. Come help me."

Chapter Thirty-three

"IT'S YOU, ISN'T IT?" Kelly asked Andi. They were sitting on the lanai loveseat with Piper lying across Kelly's lap where she could easily be petted.

"What are you talking about?" Andi asked, avoiding eye contact by looking down at Piper and scratching her ears.

"You're the one buying this house."

"Oh, you got an offer on it? Wow, that was fast." Her eyes never left Piper, her fingers stroking Piper's ears.

"Come on, now, don't play dumb. I know it's you. The house was only on the market for a few hours, and as far as I know no one came to see it. You've already seen it, so I'm figuring you're the one who wanted to buy it. Fess up."

Andi groped for a response. She decided she wasn't going to lie to Kelly ever again and looked up. "You won't believe this. My aunt found Lauren through referrals from friends. It was pure coincidence that she was the one we dealt with, honestly. I told her I was looking for commercial property for a gallery here and a small home here for me. Your house came up."

"Right."

"Well, that's exactly what happened. Of course, I gave her the street address of this house to be sure. She showed it to me on the list. To tell you the truth, I was going to go through all kinds of backstreets to be sure you didn't find out it was me until we signed the final papers. Since you figured it out already, well, I guess that's rather useless. I should've known better."

"You know confession is good for the soul. You really want this house?"

"I really, really want it. In fact, I love it and I can't wait to live here." She gazed into Kelly's eyes. "It's simply perfect...exactly what I want. Everything here calls to me and says 'home' each time."

"When I met you last year I'd never have thought that you'd be doing something like this. Seriously."

"Neither would I. I was hurting and wanted it to stop."

"And...has it?"

"It has. It definitely has."

Kelly brushed a strand of hair from Andi's brow. "I'm glad."

"I am, too. I guess if all that hadn't happened, we wouldn't have met."

"True. If Elise hadn't wanted bookcases at a time when the construction company was busy, it still wouldn't have happened."

"I'm glad it did. You're great to cuddle with."

"So are you." Kelly was quiet for a few seconds. "You know, the last thing on my mind at the time I met Elise was looking for a date. I mean Elise is cute and all that..." She grinned. "You're much cuter."

"Aww...thanks. Speaking of Aunt Elise, I think your friend Lauren's interested in her. Unless I'm mistaken and she's not..."

"Oh, yes, she is. You aren't wrong about that. I didn't realize Elise was. I guess it never occurred to me. She's old enough to be my mother."

"Yeah, I guess we don't think of parental types in that way. I think I mentioned a while back that Aunt Elise was hurt badly years ago. I didn't say who it was that did it."

"I remember that. What happened?"

"It was a nasty story. She had a long-time partner that decided to cheat on her. It was probably the worst kind of cheating there is. The other woman was a real cliché."

"No, not Elise's best friend."

"Yes, it was. So not only did she lose her partner, she lost her best friend...the one she'd normally have gone to for support. It was awful. She decided to leave relationships alone. She's had a very full life with lots of friends and all, except she had no partner."

"I'm sure her other friends tried to fix her up. I can imagine she'd be quite a catch. She's an interesting and lovely woman."

"Of course, they did. Every time Elise realized what was happening she'd politely tell the woman they set her up with that she wasn't interested in a relationship."

"I suppose it didn't take long before her friends finally gave up trying to set her up?"

"That's pretty much it. She became the favorite aunt type person. She's always been number one with me, but I'm biased. The older she got, the fewer wanted to be friends only. They wanted to settle down with someone. And she had me, as well, in the beginning. I guess that might've been some of it. I've been out of the house for a long time now so that can't be an issue any more. I guess she stopped looking."

"What happened this afternoon?"

"I could swear there was something there as soon as their eyes met. Aunt Elise blushed. We all sat around the lanai table with drinks while Lauren showed us properties on her laptop. By the way, the pictures Lauren took of your house are very nice. I would've wanted this house simply from those pictures. She's good."

"She's good alright. That's why she's been my agent for a long time now. Go on about what happened."

"Well, have you ever noticed that Lauren's laugh sounds a lot like Lauren Bacall?"

"No, I guess not. I've known her for ages and probably never paid any attention."

"She has that same throaty laugh as the actress. Anyway, my aunt adores Lauren Bacall movies. We watched a lot of them while I was growing up. I'm sure lots of lesbians were in love with her. Back to this afternoon. I thought Aunt Elise was going to be able to power solar panels as much as she was glowing every time Lauren said anything to her. I've never seen her like that."

"Did it seem mutual? Lauren has been single for quite a while now."

"It did. Lauren asked Elise to go to a banquet this evening as her guest and she accepted."

"Wow. Good for them. I'd love to see Lauren with someone nice. And Elise definitely qualifies."

"She asked me to help her pick out the right dress, too. She was a bit nervous, I think. I love seeing her like this."

"And I love just seeing you. I'm going to be sorry to see you return to New York."

"Well, I'm staying for another few days…long enough to check on gallery space with Lauren. We're going tomorrow to look at some places here in Fort Myers and one or two in Naples."

"I can't believe you're actually doing this. I mean, you're really serious."

"Of course, I am. I thought about you so much while I was in New York. All I wanted was to be free to tell you how much I cared about you. In the process, I nearly lost you. I know now that I didn't go about it the right way. I can assure you my heart was in the right place."

"I understand that. I care about you, too." Kelly pulled Andi closer.

"Very much." She gently stroked the side of Andi's face.

Andi responded by placing a kiss on Kelly's lips, turning further to deepen the kiss. She sighed as she pulled away.

"What?" Kelly asked. "I can see those wheels turning in your head."

"I have an idea." She appeared to search Kelly's eyes for a possible response before she said anything more. "I'm not sure you'll go for it."

"What kind of idea?"

"It has to do with this house." Andi paused for a second, then appeared to decide to blurt it out. "I think we should live in this house together."

"Uh…"

"Oh. My. God. I hope I didn't scare you." Andi jumped up. "I'm sorry if you think it's too much too fast."

"No, it's…"

"I mean, it hasn't been that long and you might still have reservations and…" Andi began pacing, looking at her feet the whole time. Piper got up and began running back and forth in front of her.

"Look, I…"

"I'm sorry, I shouldn't have said anything. Seriously, if you think it's too soon I'll understand."

Kelly got up and in two strides caught Andi and held her in her arms tightly. She stepped back and put a hand on each side of Andi's face, looking her in the eyes. "I didn't say that. Heck, I didn't say anything. You didn't give me a chance. I think it's a great idea."

"You do?"

"I do. If we're going to do that, I can only sell you a half interest in the house. That's final."

"All right, then, half interest. Lauren can redo the paperwork. Oh, Kelly, I just want to be here with you. That's all I want. I…"

"You…what?"

"I, uh, I'm working everything out. It's going to work. Whenever I need to be in New York I can stay at Aunt Elise's place, and this will be my home. My real home. Here. With you."

Kelly searched Andi's eyes. "Look, I have to ask one last time. You know this isn't some Park Avenue condo or a Palm Harbour place. You're absolutely positive you want to live here?"

Andi didn't waver. She looked straight back, answering her with a kiss. "I'm as sure as sure can be. Kelly, I know what I want. I love this house and I want you and care very much for you. I'm not doing this on a whim. I've been thinking about it for months and talking to Aunt Elise trying to figure out how to make it work if I came back here and found you wanted me. This house is quite frankly the icing on the cake. I planned to buy a house here anyway, but this one, well, this one's perfect."

Kelly pulled her back into her arms and stroked her back gently with one hand. "I do want you. I want you very much. And I care very much for you, too." Kelly couldn't tell her she loved her. Not yet. But she knew she would, and soon. She knew in her heart that Andi was going to be part of her very own happy ever after and let out a little sigh.

As Andi snuggled further into Kelly's arms, Kelly knew here was where they both belonged. "Welcome home," she whispered.

THE END

About BJ Phillips

I've been writing practically since I've been reading. People who knew me well knew my biggest dream and biggest fear was writing a whole book. That fear of failure. I had poetry published in my school literary magazine and a funny story in my work professional magazine. I wrote training materials for work and helped friends write their resumes, feeling that was at least writing. I had the beginnings of fantasy stories, mysteries, and love stories all sitting in folders and notebooks.

In the summer of 2013 I saw the National Novel Writing Month (NaNoWriMo) challenge. If you're not familiar with it, the challenge is to write 50,000 words in 30 days. The day after Thanksgiving that year, I posted 51,000 words and a complete story was born. It needed a lot of work, but it was there. That story was the bones of Hurricane Season, my debut novel, which will be out in spring 2016.

Early in 2014, I heard about a new program through the Golden Crown Literary Society (GCLS) called the Writing Academy. It's a one year program aimed at new writers or writers who want to improve their skills. I'm proud to be part of the very first graduating class.

The Writing Academy was life-changing. I started looking at myself as an author, not just as someone who happens to write. I retired the beginning of 2015. I became a full-time writer of stories and finally finished my first book the end of July 2015.

I live in Florida with my partner, a retired police officer, Maya the Yorkie, and Piper the Chihuahua in an honest-to-goodness resort—it says so on the sign out front. When I'm not writing, we love sitting out on the front porch with the "kids" and chatting with neighbors and friends who like to come by and visit. I'm an avid reader of anything that strikes my fancy and I love puzzles – like logic problems, Sudoku or word finds. I also like to take walks, go to flea markets, sketch, and crochet. Okay, I'm also addicted to several TV shows, mostly mysteries and cop shows. Thank goodness for the DVR!

I'm very excited about becoming part of the Desert Palm Press family. I have two more books in the pipeline right now, a murder mystery and another romance.

Connect with BJ

Email: bjphillipswrites@gmail.com

Website: www.bjphillipsauthor.com

Twitter: https//twitter.com/bjwrites01

Other Books from Desert Palm Press

BJ Phillips

Hurricane Season

ISBN: 9781942976134

Shawn Richards (aka S.K. Richardson) is a romance author. She's had her heart broken badly again and is done with love. Ditching San Francisco, she moves back home to Southwest Florida to get her feet back under her and finish her latest novel.

Carrie Alexander is a huge S.K. Richardson fan, but has no idea what she looks like. She does, however, like the looks of the new neighbor down the street, Shawn Richards.

Drawn to each other as friends, Shawn still tries to keep some distance despite what she's beginning to feel for Carrie. Carrie isn't the kind of woman you just have a fun night with and then move on. Carrie's the kind you fall in love with and make love to, and live happily ever after with—but she just can't let herself trust her heart yet. After all, the last time she fell for one of her fans, it ended badly.

Carrie is looking for 'happy ever after' just like in all those romance novels she reads. Shawn could be the one, or maybe Carrie's fooling herself and there's really no such thing as all that romantic stuff in Shawn's books.

Shawn is afraid she can't deliver on that 'happy ever after' she knows Carrie wants—and she wants, too, truth be told. Destiny might have given them a push when Carrie tripped at the local grocery store and literally fell into Shawn's arms. But fear could cost Shawn the woman of her dreams.

AJ Adaire

FRIEND SERIES

Sunset Island

ISBN: 9781301136629

Ren Madison is certain her life couldn't be more perfect. She owns a private island with an Inn off the coast of Maine. She treasures her loving relationship with her older brother Jack, his wife, Marie, and dotes on her niece Laura. She has a passionate and supportive relationship with her partner, Brooke, and a successful business that doesn't require her undivided attention allowing her ample time to pursue her true passion, painting.

Ren's idyllic world crumbles when Brooke dies. Friends and family worry that Ren may never fully recover from her loss.

Dr. Lindy Caprini, a multi-lingual professor, is looking for an artist to illustrate the book she is writing comparing fairy tales from around the world. To make working together on the book easier, Lindy takes a year sabbatical and leaves friends, home, and boyfriend in Pennsylvania and moves to Ren's island. Ren soon discovers that the beautiful and mischievous Lindy is a talented author and a witty conversationalist. Their collaboration on the book leads to a close, light hearted, and flirtatious friendship. Will their collaboration end there?

The Interim (a novelette)
ISBN: 9781311099051

Devastated that her partner cheated, Melanie flees to a new job in Maine, where she meets Ren Madison. Ren is dealing with issues of her own after losing her partner Brooke in a plane crash

What happens in the interim after one relationship ends and you're really ready to love again? For Ren Madison, Melanie was what happened.

The Interim fills in the details of Ren Madison's life on Sunset Island after Brooke but before Lindy.

Awaiting My Assignment
ISBN: 9781310825248

Bernie was a liar. Amanda learned that much when she caught her lover cheating the first time. Upon discovering a second indiscretion, Amanda vows there will never be another. She leaves the relationship, fleeing to her friend Dana in New York State. While staying at Dana's home, Amanda meets and falls in love with a wonderful woman named Mallory.

Amanda is ready to move on. However, the consistently surprising Bernie isn't finished yet. Amanda learns of Bernie's rudest betrayal yet when she receives a package from her recently deceased ex-lover. A very surprising revelation and one final request are contained therein. The favor comes with a gift that delivers dramatic and life-altering changes, not only to Amanda's life, but to the lives of her closest friends and new partner as well.

Anything Your Heart Desires

ISBN: 978131163912

"Whoa—lesbians!" That was Stacy Alexander's first thought as she observes the group of women in the new shop across the street kiss each other in greeting. Stacy had been staring out her apartment window trying to think of a motive for the death of the character she'd killed off in her mystery novel. Ah ha—extortion! What could be a better reason for the murder of my heroine than being blackmailed because she's a lesbian? Now all I need is a lesbian to teach me about the 'lesbian lifestyle.'

That's where policewoman Jo Martin enters the picture. Jo has two rules by which she religiously lives her life: never get involved with someone already in a relationship and never, ever date a straight woman. As Jo and Stacy collaborate on the novel, will Stacy want to gain a more intimate knowledge of the topic, and will Jo hold steadfastly to her rules?

One Day Longer Than Forever

ISBN: 9781310847738

Dr. Kate Martin needs a vacation after a failed romance with her business partner nearly ruins her. Lee Foster is recovering from her first lesbian relationship that self-destructed when her partner moved several states away, leaving her behind.

Two failed romances, a double-booked vacation cabin, and a blizzard—will fate intervene again and turn a passionate affair with a stranger, into something more?

It's Complicated

ISBN: 9781311122964

Victoria Brannigham had a guilty pleasure. Every day she would take a detour, sit on the boardwalk, and wait. She tried not to covet what could never be hers. Beverly McMannis was lonely, until she discovered another lesbian on the island. Bev eagerly embraced the growing friendship with her neighbor. Victoria was honest with Bev right from the start; explaining that she wasn't free to explore their attraction. Bev promised to honor the boundaries. Love isn't always easy, sometimes it's complicated...especially when she doesn't know you're still being faithful.

Desert Palm Press

I Love My Life
ISBN: 9781311310002

Betrayal by her former partner sends Chris Baxter fleeing to Maine. To escape the monotony of staring at the four walls of her isolated cabin, she enrolls in a sailing class. A chance pairing with Stephanie Kincaid and her cohorts, Tina and Terry, offers an opportunity for new friendship. Their shared homework assignment might offer Chris the potential for more than just knowledge of navigation.

An urgent message interrupts the classmates' sailing vacation along the coast of Maine. While Chris rushes back to her twin's bedside, the others remain onboard to sail back to their homeport. Will the revelations from her ex, her sister, and her family, change everything in the new life that Chris has rebuilt?

Desert Palm Press

Journey to You
ISBN: 9781311571854

What do you do if you are one of the few who remain alive after a mysterious, flu-like virus claims most of the global population? This is a question Kim Robins and Peri Henderson must answer when the world changes and society falls apart.

Violent gangs of looters make it unsafe to remain in the city. Hoping to improve their chances for survival, Kim and Peri decide to hike into the remote forest area of Maine.

Dangerous circumstances along the trail cause the women to join forces with another hiker and her dog. The longtime friends and their new companions set off on a daunting trek filled with both menacing and kindhearted survivors.

In this romantic adventure, the real question to be answered is, will this journey bring each of the women the happiness and safety she seeks?

Don't Forget

ISBN: 9781942976318

In 1986, Jamie Parker falls in love. What could be bad about that? Nothing except that the object of her affection is Val DiLeona, friend and fellow administrator in the same school district. If Jamie has misinterpreted that Val has similar feelings, confessing her affection could result in the end of their friendship. Then there is the little matter of the consequences at work. Outing herself as a lesbian could result in her losing her job.

Nearly thirty years later, in 2016, Jamie meets ambulance driver, Kelly, in a hospital waiting room. Upon learning how long Jamie and her partner have been together, Kelly asks Jamie to tell her their story. As Jamie begins, neither woman can imagine the impact their casual conversation will have on their lives, and the lives of those they love.

TJ Whittle

Without Your Courage

ISBN: 9781310147548

What does courage look like to you? Is it a young girl facing an unwanted marriage? Does it echo the fears of a spouse exposing their secret? Is it the strength of a young woman protecting her unborn child? Perhaps it's as simple as a first kiss. Without Your Courage takes us to Auckland, New Zealand and the surrounding countryside, to join the lives of four strong women.

1940s. Violet and Charlotte form a beautiful friendship while John is away at war. What will happen when he returns?

Present Day. An accident introduces Ella and Gemma, who struggle to define their new friendship across the barrier of age. Four women with their lives entwined. Will they find the love they seek?

An Empty Stool

ISBN: 9781942976349

Trauma glues you to your seat. Don't move, don't make any noise, it's safer to be unseen. And really, watching the world through a lens isn't so bad. You're doing ok till, one day, someone notices you and makes contact. That first little nudge is so shocking that even your favourite café stool isn't safe anymore. But when Hope keeps calling, what do you do?

S.L. Kassidy

Please Baby

ISBN: 9781311485137

Jayce Newton's life is going downhill after she rescues her little niece from an awful situation. She plans to hold onto her niece and gain custody of her, but there are some factors against her. Her girlfriend doesn't want the baby around. Her mother wants to take the baby from her, and her brother has disappeared. Things only seem to get worse when Gus Tucker comes into her life.

Gus Tucker's life isn't going much better. She recently divorced her wife and moved into a new home. She's looking forward to a new start and spending time with her sister. Before she can do that, though, she ends up causing trouble for Jayce Newton, getting her fired from her job and kicked out of her home. She tries to make it up to Jayce by taking her in during her time of need. Now, it's just a struggle to see if they're able to coexist in the same house with a baby between them.

SCARRED SERIES

Scarred for Life
ISBN: 9781310171352

Dane Wolfe is a loner. Forsaken by her family and betrayed by people close to her, she has lost all faith in people and spends her days wandering the streets with no direction or meaning. She drifts through life, existing and nothing more. Nicole Cardell is a successful attorney. She has too much faith in people and is being taken advantage of by her boyfriend, Tyler, Dane's cousin. She's tired of his selfish ways and tosses him out. The bad relationship leaves her questioning her judgment. Circumstances bring Dane and Nicole together and a friendship brings them closer. They're able to heal each other and bring balance to each other's lives. Their peace is shattered when family causes trouble and tears them apart. Will they find their path back to each other and to the love that was slowly growing?

New Cuts, Old Wounds
ISBN: 9781310217289

In this sequel to *Scarred for Life*, Nicole Cardell and Dane Wolfe have been together for a year. They are doing their best to move forward with their relationship and open up to each other. It's time to meet family members. Dane's nervous about meeting Nicole's family, but she's even more nervous about Nicole meeting her family. Nicole is eager for both. Nicole thinks Dane should bond with her family while Dane thinks she needs to get as far away from them as possible. The Wolfe family seems to agree with Dane, but keep inviting her to things and Nicole keeps accepting the invites. Will family make or break Dane and Nicole?

Bandages
ISBN: 9781942976103

Nicole and Dane return in the third installment of the *Scarred* series. Life is good. The musician gave the lawyer a ring, a not-engagement ring, a promise; this is forever. But, they both still had some growing and healing to work through.

Healing is strange. There are those days when the bandage falls off on its own and you think you're good to go. Days when laughter comes easy and you forget the past. And there are days when the past doesn't want to be forgotten; you still need a stitch or a cast to hold yourself together. There are even relapses when the poisonous past needs release.

Share their journey through eighteen short stories of play, passion, and a deepening partnership. You'll enjoy the journey as much as where it leads.

First Degree Burns
ISBN: 9781942976257
Dane and Nicole are back in this sequel to Bandages. Nicole arranges a camping trip for Dane to meet Nicole's father's side of the family. Nicole is trying to move their relationship forward, but things do not go the way that she planned. Dane has a lot more excitement on her first camping trip than either of them thought. Hopefully, it doesn't ruin what they have already.

Note to Readers:

Thank you for reading a book from Desert Palm Press. We have made every effort to edit this book. However, typos do slip in. If you find an error in the text, please email lee@desertpalmpress.com so the issue can be corrected.

We appreciate you as a reader and want to ensure you enjoy the reading process. We would like you to consider posting a review on your preferred media sites such as Amazon, Smashwords, Bella Books, Goodreads, Tumblr, Twitter, Facebook, and/or your blog or website.

For more information on upcoming releases, author interviews, contest, giveaways and more, please sign up for our newsletter and visit us as at Desert Palm Press - www.desertpalmpress.com and "Like" us on Facebook: Desert Palm Press.

Bright Blessings